C000091761

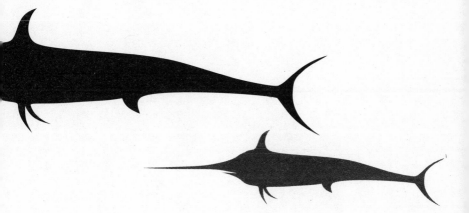

The Swordfish

HUGO CLAUS

The Swordfish

*Translated from the Flemish
and with an Introduction by*
RUTH LEVITT

PETER OWEN • London
UNESCO Publishing • Paris

PETER OWEN PUBLISHERS
73 Kenway Road London SW5 0RE
Peter Owen books are distributed in the USA by
Dufour Editions Inc. Chester Springs PA 19425–0007

Translated from the Flemish *De Zwaardvis*
© Hugo Claus 1989
English translation © Ruth Levitt 1996
First published in Great Britain 1996

UNESCO Collection of Representative Works

All Rights Reserved.
No part of this publication may be reproduced in any
form or by any means without the written permission of
the publishers

ISBN 0–7206–0985–2
UNESCO ISBN 92–3–103277–1

A catalogue record for this book is available from
the British Library

Printed and made in Great Britain by Biddles
of Guildford and King's Lynn

For Oscar with my thanks for his *Italian Concerto*

Introduction

Each March during 'Book Week', a scheme sponsored by the Foundation for the Joint Promotion of the Dutch Book (CPNB), bookshops in the Netherlands give away copies of a specially written new work of literature in Dutch. In 1989 the work was *The Swordfish* by the Belgian writer Hugo Claus. A total of 450,000 were distributed in that way, and since then the publisher, De Bezige Bij in Amsterdam, has sold over 9,000 copies. The work has already been translated into French, German, Portuguese, Norwegian, Danish and Swedish.

Hugo Claus, now 67, is the leading Belgian writer of his generation. He has written prolifically, creating an important and original oeuvre of almost one hundred works that encompasses poetry,[1] novels and short stories,[2] and plays.[3]

1. The complete poems have been published as *Gedichten 1948–1993*. The poems in English translations include 'In a Harbour' (1981), *The Sign of the Hamster* (1986) and *Selected Poems 1953–73* (1986)

He has also written essays and screenplays and directed films, as well as being an active painter and draughtsman. Throughout his career his writings have achieved recognition and been awarded prestigious prizes in Belgium and the Netherlands. He has been regarded as a candidate for the Nobel literature prize for several years.

He grew up in Bruges in the Flemish-speaking part of Belgium. During the early 1950s he was in Paris and then in Rome before moving to Ghent, where he lived from 1955 to 1966. He next spent four years in the Ardennes and transferred to Amsterdam for most of the 1970s, before returning to Ghent. In recent years he and his wife Veerle de Wit have made their main home in France in the Vaucluse, while keeping a base in Antwerp and making frequent trips abroad.

Claus was eighteen years old when his first collection of poetry was published in 1947. Three years later his first prose work appeared. From 1949 to 1955 he edited the poetry journal *Tijd en Mens*. At that time he was associated with the Existentialist and Surrealist movements, particularly through his involvement with the 'Vijftigers', a group of Dutch artists in Paris, and COBRA, an international association of artists in Copenhagen, Brussels and Amsterdam. Influences included Antonin Artaud and Pierre Alechinsky. For two years he was active in film-making at the Cinecittà in Rome with his first wife, the actress Elly Overzier.

The two prose works by Hugo Claus that have achieved the greatest acclaim are *De verwondering* (*Wonderment*, 1962) and *Het verdriet van België* (*The Sorrow of Belgium*, 1983). *Wonderment* has been called 'a masterpiece and a milestone

---

2. The novels translated into English are *The Duck Hunt* (1955) and *The Sorrow of Belgium* (1990); the translated short stories include 'The Lieutenant' (1964) and 'The Black Emperor' (1970)

3. The plays in English translation include *A Bride in the Morning* (1960), *Friday* (1972), *Two-Brush Painting* (1980), *Back Home* and *The Life and Works of Leopold II* (1984) and *Four Works for Theatre* (1990)

in the history of the Flemish novel [. . .] in which three texts are plaited together. The main character's, De Rijckel's, psychiatrist has set him "homework", whereby he must create distance between himself and his traumas. Covertly, he also keeps two other pieces of writing: a "notebook", airing the problems of Flemish nationhood, the youth movement, collaboration and repression; and a diary, a rancorous, discontinuous commentary of the fictive, false structure of the "homework" assignment. Writing hasn't given him a "crystal-clear journey" towards an identity.'[4]

The Sorrow of Belgium, written over a period of ten years, is generally regarded as Claus's magnum opus. It tells the story of a boy in Flanders in the difficult years of war and peace between 1939 and 1947. 'In a bewildering interplay of fact and fiction, Claus recounts the story of his own youth and his first steps towards becoming a writer. At the same time it is a picaresque novel, in which the boy who began as the victim of the lies and treachery of adults becomes a cheat and a liar. [. . .] A more brutal exposé of the spiritual poverty of both Flemish society and its intellectuals has seldom been presented.'[5]

Claus writes with great originality, and it is unwise to try to pin down his literary productions into any ready-made categories. Although such terms as 'experimental' and 'avant-garde' have frequently been applied to his output, the persistently unpredictable style and approach tend to defy labelling. His creativity is innovatory, iconoclastic and energetic. He has absorbed a rich literary inheritance, finding the classical writers Seneca, Euripides and Sophocles to be particular inspirations. He has produced adaptations of their creations as well as reworking Shakespeare's *Sonnets* and translating Dylan

4. Hugo Bousset: 'Writing to a Personal Myth', *Image of an Age* (exh. cat., Palais des Beaux-Arts, Brussels, 1991), pp. 245, 373

5. Paul Claes: 'Claus the Chameleon', *The Low Countries 1993–94* (Stichting Ons Erfdeel, Rekkem, 1995), pp. 22, 23

Thomas into Flemish. He is an enthusiastic explorer in the realms of language and myth, a pioneer in the treatment of narrative. His writings have addressed large and small themes, invoking satire at times, as well as profound despair. He has invented explosive, violent language on occasions; he has found meanings in the magical and spiritual.

The Swordfish is a short novel, yet it is richly engaged with many significant concerns. It is ostensibly the story of a summer moment in the lives, fantasies and sensibilities of a young, headstrong boy, his now-single mother, the local village headmaster and a vet who has fallen on hard times. Ironically, and with a masterfully light touch, Claus brings the reader into close contact with such perplexing matters as loss, truth, religion, passion, desire and crime.

Ruth Levitt
London, March 1996

How will it be when the swordfish draws near
Borne on the swelling tides of barbaric dreams?

Maurice Gilliams

Sibylle Verhegge is sitting on a deckchair on the terrace, in her bikini, painting her toenails mother-of-pearl; eight months ago she was still Sibylle Ghyselen. Bees buzz around her, attracted by the sweet smell of the suntan oil. In her mother's opinion, it's high time she started a new life in a large town and forgot all about the unfortunate interlude of her marriage and her time in the country. Sibylle has a vague idea what the house is worth, but what's the going rate for agricultural land here, and how much is there?

'How big is our estate?' she had once asked Gerard, as he bounced their little seven-months-old son, Martin – gurgling, wrinkled, plump – on his knees. Gerard said nothing and laid the child back in the cot. He had that familiar bitter twist around his lipless mouth. He was convinced she was laughing at him again, and he remembered what he had said a few times of late: 'One can take only so much. . . .'

'Estate?' he said, over the child's howls. It was years ago.

'Property, I mean.'

'Say property then.'

'How big is our property?' But that sounded wrong too. She had been there when the surveyor measured it, so she must have known how much there was. Gerard had had more hair then, though he was as slim as when he walked out on her all those years later. He had marched through the corn beside the toothy dwarf of a farmer who sold them the land, striding and counting out loud, ill at ease, elegant, not at home in the country as Martin now was, hauling planks about in the orchard.

After that, Gerard never walked about the property except with business friends, who trailed after him in their tailored suits and expensive shoes as he pointed out the views and drew their attention to an immense lime tree beside the road. He called it 'my tree'.

The council had decreed that the lime would have to be cut down as it cast too much shadow over the field belonging to the town clerk, who anyway had trouble turning his tractor there. Gerard claimed he had overruled the mayor in order to save the giant tree; he had slipped him some cash of course, much too much, but he could afford it. What mattered was being able to say: 'My lime tree, my property, my soap works, my firm Olympia, my fertilizers, my lethal pesticides, my wife Sibylle, whom I shall desert because of a foolish misunderstanding, my little son Martin with his long, wild hair and amber eyes.'

Two hectares, say? Is green-belt land more expensive or less nowadays, as you can't build houses on it? She missed

Gerard at such moments, his liking for precision, order, quick decisions, his enthusiasm. The business friends drank whisky on the terrace and admired the orchard, about which Gerard invariably said: 'Christ has not yet passed by here.'

Sibylle had thought the expression quaint, rooted in medieval sayings, until she discovered it was the title of an Italian film.

One reason why her mother thinks she should leave this area is that Martin hasn't settled in at the village school. 'He's turning into a country bumpkin more and more every day,' says her mother. Sibylle can't tell whether Martin is content at the school. The last few weeks he has been very anxious, obsessed about getting in to school on time.

What's the house likely to be worth? Would people pay that bit more for it because the living-room floor is tiled in special black stone, because a panoramic window looks out on to the orchard and fields, because the open fireplace is extra large and copied from a typical Brabant farmhouse? Gerard wanted that open fireplace. The useless gaping hole in her living-room seems disturbing and unsafe to her, smoke-blackened and empty, with its dusty wicker basket of logs. Because it served a somewhat ambivalent purpose? Just like her?

'My marriage was a mistake,' she said recently to her mother, who was only too glad to hear it. 'I have to have a husband who can relate. Who doesn't always take what I say literally, who doesn't instantly get cross if I mean something well but express it badly, who can take a joke, so I don't always have to be begging: do forgive me, I'm sorry, but I meant it differently. . . .'

That open fireplace. 'My open fireplace. My billiard room, my sycamore on the lawn in front of the wall!' What else must a man of substance have accomplished in his life? Bring up a son, plant a tree, and something else . . . what is the third? Lay down a cellar of wine? I'm beginning to forget everything. They all notice but no one says anything to me about it. What do they say among themselves? 'Sibylle Ghyselen is getting fat, flabby, heavy, lazy; she's forgetful; you get like that when you're alone, want to be on your own, have to be on your own.' Advertise: 'Restored villa. No – country house, with rustic charm, two marble bathrooms, double glazing, fully carpeted, large fireplace, wide fireplace, open fireplace. Private spring. Spring with own water.'

You can hear the gushing sound of the spring from the terrace. A Coca-Cola bottle fills up immediately if you hold it underneath the spring. Ice-cold water rushing over the old mossy green stone steps between the bamboo canes.

A source of income, according to Sibylle's mother. Last week in the kitchen she said it was a shame that such an abundant supply of water didn't bring them in anything. You could launch a new brand of mineral water on the market, as long as you provided a miracle.

'What kind of miracle?' said Martin fiercely.

'Well, if a couple of boys at school announced one day that a saint had been seen at our spring.'

'Which saint, Gran?'

'It doesn't matter which. Why not St Martin? Is there one?'

Sibylle caught the unusually menacing look Martin gave his grandmother, a look of disgust and rage.

'What's the matter, Martin?'

'Nothing, Mum.'

Her mother didn't notice anything of course, and chattered on: 'Martin, wouldn't you be pleased if a mineral water was named after you? St Martin's Water, with little bubbles.'

'Pleased!' The boy screamed, going bright red. He raced out, as usual into the orchard, where he flailed his arms about and hit out at the silver birches with his plastic sword.

Advertise. Phone the solicitor. Leave. Perhaps my mother is right after all. The countryside is for cattle.

The sun is now shining straight into her face; the suntan oil runs into her eyes. Move the parasol. Even that seems too difficult, as impractical as tidying the bathroom, pulling up weeds, chopping wood for the damned open fireplace, repairing the thatched roof, as Richard is doing, seated astride the ridge of the barn. He is not working; he is holding on to the wrought iron weathercock.

'I don't want the roof thatched with reeds, Gerard.'
'But darling, everyone does, all the barns round here have a reed roof.'
'I want straw, proper straw, like it used to be.'
He muttered something about how much higher the insurance would be.
She had expected more opposition, hoped for it. But straw it was, half a metre thick, in flattened bundles, a cornfield on the roof, with an unnatural golden yellow glow when the sun shone on it.
A week later it had faded and turned lifeless when they sprayed it with something to prevent it catching fire. She felt abandoned, betrayed.
'But darling, it had to be done, otherwise it'd be much too dangerous.'
'So what if it's dangerous? So what if it catches fire!'
He looked incredulous, bitter.
'I'm sorry,' she said. 'What I mean is, even if everything caught fire, we'd still have each other.'
'Try pulling your mother's leg,' he snarled.

From the straw roof, Richard can see her shoulders burning because no one moves the parasol, her breasts in the bikini top that is too small, the creases above her hips, the four, five, ten grey hairs that have surfaced on the crown of her head.

If Irene was there now, Sibylle would ask for a glass

of orange juice, but the maid has gone to her sister's wedding in Waregem. Tonight she will be groped all over by an excited wedding guest.

'Oh no, Madam, I'll take good care, it'll be up to here and no further.'

'To where, Irene?'

Irene indicates a boundary above her knees with two chubby outstretched fingers.

'No further, Irene?'

'Madam, really!' High-pitched giggling.

Sibylle dreams the same dream about Irene again. The girl enters an unfamiliar room with plush curtains and receding walls and undresses carelessly, as though she is preparing to go to sleep in her own solitary single bed. She wears gossamer peach-coloured underwear. She leans over, hands on her knees, and waits, as if she is going to be executed. A woman appears in the mirror on the front of the wardrobe, a taller, darker and more ornamented wardrobe than the one in Sibylle's bedroom. All she has on is a very short T-shirt and lace-up boots. She has no face, although she does have Sibylle's abundant chestnut hair. The woman is overwhelmed by an immense feeling of compassion, and she nestles against Irene's thin back and sobs, until her mouth finds Irene's left nipple.

The sheep are fighting each other in the orchard, biting into each other's fleeces, knocking their skulls together; it sounds like dry branches cracking. Now and then a guineafowl takes flight, speckled grey and white like a shred of checked cloth. The goat Bokkie stands on her hind legs and nibbles at branches in an apple tree. Martin is standing next to Bokkie talking to her, leaning on the rickety cross made of two planks, which he has been hauling around with him the whole afternoon.

Yesterday Richard claimed that the reason Bokkie was twitchy was because she sensed her own death approaching and could already imagine the butcher's knife.

18

'But Bokkie's never seen a butcher's knife.'

'Her parents did, Martin.'

Martin doesn't understand.

'She got that fear of the knife at birth,' said Richard. Seeing that Martin was confused, Sibylle said, 'Richard, stop that foolish talk.' 'Yes, Madam,' said Richard immediately, his turquoise eyes glassy, his voice deep and enticing, like a drunken man's.

Sibylle perspires freely now; her forehead gleams.

She is waiting for someone. Something. A fluttering. For a magpie to fall out of the clear blue sky. She imagines putting on her dinner jacket, with a white checked shirt of Gerard's; her hair is combed back and shines from the gel; she studies herself in the wardrobe mirror and invites Irene playfully for a waltz. Her soul evaporates and leaves her ridiculous, useless, waltzing body.

Just beneath the tiled roof above the living-room, wasps are busy making a clump, a nest, a fragile tangle. It reminds her of Gerard's impetuousness. In the factories, at the office, here in the living-room, in the hall, the day he walked out and had to restrain himself from making a dash for the Porsche.

'For good?' Sibylle had asked.

'I think so.'

'Just like that?' Oh, that pedantic, fault-finding tone she can't keep out of her voice.

'Not just like that, Sibylle.'

'But I haven't done anything wrong, have I?'

'You know very well what you've done. But I'm not saying another word about it.'

'But you haven't said anything yet.'

'And I'm not going to either.'

'Can't I be forgiven?'

'You can't help it.'

Did he say that? Wasn't it rather 'You can't be helped'? She had failed to listen properly, at the very moment when her family, her child, her house, everything was at stake. Gerard bored her.

Nodding seriously, Martin says something else to the goat. He hitches the planks up on his back and hauls them onwards. He is dressed up like an old man or a wizard, talking to himself.

The cat Perry wanders round the lawn; ten molehills appeared there overnight. Soon it will bring a mole on to the terrace and drop it at Sibylle's feet, the bloody red snout pointing towards her.

The police commissioner sat fixed in his chair but leaned forward across the desk to scrutinize the man, right down to his ankles. Lippens, the policeman, shoved the man in the back.

'Sit there,' said the police commissioner, his high, girlish voice surprisingly light for his cumbersome, muscular bulk.

Lippens took the handcuffs off; the man scarcely noticed. He chewed air with his yellow teeth and put his hand into his trousers pocket, in search of cigarettes or a packet of tobacco. Lippens immediately pulled the hand out, large, thickly veined, with scratched fingers, and the man then thrust it towards the police commissioner. He stared at his hand as though checking whether or not it trembled.

'Sit down, I say.'

The police commissioner wore the impenetrable expression he had learnt long ago at police training school. His wife had never been able to get used to it.

He read out a number of statements. The man nodded as he had learnt to, he accepted all stipulations, all sections. He wasn't wearing socks. Spots of blood were visible on his right ankle. The police commissioner thought he heard faint squelching sounds from the blood-stained shoes.

'We've plenty of time,' said the police commissioner. Nowadays the deserted town produced few delinquents. Since the textile industry had been bled dry the young people went off to the large town. The only appointment in his diary was with Clara, a half-deaf prostitute, who gave the neighbourhood problems with her twelve cats. She was waiting for a telling-off in one of the police station's five cells.

'Enough time to turn over a new leaf, sir' said Lippens.

The man continued to move his mouth with its chapped lips and protruding teeth; he swallowed repeatedly.

'Right,' said the police commissioner, 'say something.'

'What do you want to know?'

'Start at the beginning.'

The man shuffled his feet uneasily. Lippens leaned casually against the wall with his hand on his holster. The St Servatius church clocks began to chime. The police commissioner reluctantly remembered that he had to go to some sort of concert at the church next Sunday, that the Governor was expected for the Culture Weekend. The prospect of having to be there without his wife made him irritable. Self-pity welled up in him. 'Yesterday morning you went to work at Mrs Ghyselen's.'

'I'd rather . . .'

'You don't "rather" anything here,' said Lippens.

'Florent.' The police commissioner pointed to the half-

22

full ashtray by his green mat, which was the green of billiard-table felt. Lippens emptied the ashtray out of the window.

'Sir,' said the man, 'can't I get a little drop of something here? I'll pay for it right away.'

Lippens sniggered triumphantly. The police commissioner said, 'Listen, I have no intention of sitting here until this evening. Although we have noted all this. . . .' Why shouldn't he sit here until this evening? When his wife had still been able to walk, they went down to the Excelsior on Sunday afternoons to play cards. His wife usually won. He had been proud of that.

'You went to work at Mrs Ghyselen's.'

'For nothing,' said the man automatically.

'Moonlighting,' said the police commissioner. 'We're not stupid. But you needn't worry about that, that's not our department. So. You were working around the house. Working on what?'

'On the roof,' said the man.

'The whole day?'

'Yes. And I even made a little cap out of a handkerchief because I thought I'd get sunstroke.'

'Where's that handkerchief?' asked Lippens.

'Back in my bag. Julia always put it in my bag with my Thermos and sandwiches. She is always worried that I'll run out of something.'

'She is worried,' the police commissioner repeated in a singsong voice, and thought: How long will we go on playing this interminably repetitive game, with me as the well-meaning father and Lippens as the hothead?

'On the roof?' he asked. 'Until when?'

'I don't know any more, I was too drunk. I had to be careful when I crawled down the ladder. I thought, if I fall, I'll land gently on that pile of straw.'

'And did you leave then?'

'First of all I wanted to say goodbye to Madam Sibylle,

23

but she must have been in her bathroom. I found the little one, but he was in a mood again. So I said to him, "Boy, if you were my responsibility I'd beat you on your bare backside." That boy is being brought up by her and her mother; it's not healthy.'

'And you know all about what's healthy,' said Lippens, maintaining the puerile role of nasty policeman.

'As much as you do,' said the man. 'At least as much as you do.'

'Very well,' said the police commissioner.

'The little one is a good chap,' said the man, 'but he has moods, you can't do a thing about them. He always wants to have his own way, like her.'

'How do you mean, like her? Like Mrs Ghyselen? Or like Julia?'

'No, not like Julia. Please.' The tall, anguished man jerked so suddenly that the chair creaked violently. He half stood up. His face, inches from his interrogator's, had something obsequious and cunning about it.

'One little lager, Mr Commissioner, on me.'

'This isn't a pub,' said Lippens.

'How did you know that Mrs Ghyselen was in the bathroom? Could you see from outside?'

'No.'

'You're frowning,' said Lippens. He blew his acrid cigarette smoke into the room.

'Open your eyes when I'm talking to you,' said the police commissioner. It sounded like a gentle caution among friends at the card table. He saw the rough lout Lippens thinking: Our boss isn't the man he was anymore. He used to seize suspects by their hair in this room, kick them and roar that he'd wring the juice out of their balls if they didn't tell him what he wanted to hear. He's feebler now, handicapped since his wife's illness. So much so, dammit, that he's even handling the outcast in front of him with kid gloves, that

24

wreck who studied at university, got a diploma, according to the information in the file there, had a practice and made money like water from sick cows, poodles with colds, castrating tom cats, all round the Waasland, and then couldn't keep his hands off women, caused them to bleed, and then fled to Holland where they are intolerably tolerant about everything that questions proper values, and followed that with the greatest mutilation, life itself. That's what Lippens is thinking, thought the police commissioner.

'Were you drunk?' asked the police commissioner.

'When?'

'When you left work?'

'Much earlier.'

The St Servatius clocks could be heard.

'Are you going to interrogate Madam Sibylle too?' the man asked.

'Not me. My deputy.'

'Is that necessary? She has enough misery as it is.'

'There won't be any misery provided she has nothing to hide.'

In his imagination the police commissioner saw Lippens typing a report on the typewriter on his own desk. 'For the attention of the Chief of Police. Confidential. The work and discipline of the force are being threatened by the Commissioner's laxity.'

The man moved his lips like a fish, screwed his eyes shut.

'I even made a cross yesterday morning,' he said.

'Crossed yourself? Were you saying grace?'

'No, for the little one. A cross with planks from a broken wardrobe in the barn. I said to him. "A cross, dammit, Martin, but you've just got a silver sword from your Gran." "Please Richard," he said. "And don't tell Mum." So I say, "All right, but you'll have to raid your money box." As a joke, of course. But five minutes later he was standing there with a hundred franc note. A tip.'

'Tip! You could say that,' said Lippens.

'They've always been glad to see me there,' said the man as though he was taking his leave. He rubbed the nape of his neck.

'This time you've gone too far, friend,' said the police commissioner.

'Even though you've had all the chances in the world,' said Lippens. 'More than most.'

The man's neck and shoulders were ravaged by shooting pains. He stopped rubbing and whispered, 'I must have sugar. Or a pint. Sugar. Otherwise I'm going to pass out.' He opened wide his feline green-blue eyes, as though responding to a silent command. There were little amber-coloured flecks in the corners of his eyes, like the resin that leaks out of a tree in the sunshine.

Martin would have preferred to ascend the hills like Clint Eastwood, the hero of the boys at school, with large, sure strides, hands stroking the revolvers at his hips. But that would be heresy with a cross on your shoulders. The wish belonged to an earlier time, before he knew anything about Jesus and before Miss Dora has given him the book that he was reading furtively, in the secrecy of his room, and almost knew by heart.

He shuffles warily through the dry grass, as he has seen Jesus do on television, dragging his feet, worn out, but still going as fast as possible because he has to reach the hill of Goliath before the others, specially before Our Lady and her sister Magdalen, who can't begin crying at the foot of the cross until the star is hanging there. Meanwhile, the silver-helmeted Roman soldiers thrash his back with sticks. His skin ought to have been bare, with scarlet weals, but Mum wouldn't allow that. She worries that he'll catch cold even in this heat. Mum is against God. She learnt that from Dad, who is a heathen and has a girlfriend.

The cross is heavy. He ought to ask Richard to saw a bit off the ends, but Richard was so taken with his handiwork it would break his heart. A heart can break. Jesus, this cross is heavy. Not as heavy as Jesus's was, of course. He kept falling down and they had to drag him the last few metres. His cross was made by his father, or rather, by the husband of Jesus's mother, who was a carpenter.

Invisible Pharisees mock him as he arrives at the orchard fence. 'Aha, here comes the reindeer!' Achilles the postman, Rick the baker and various boys from his class are among the Pharisees and other cowardly Jews. They pick their noses and flick the balls of snot at his face. What was that word again? They scorned him. 'Hey, are you the reindeer? Don't you need to grow a bit taller first? And what kind of beard is that, reindeer?'

Martin had made the beard out of strands of grey wool he had stolen from Mum's cupboard and stuck on his cheeks with extra strong stuff for leather, and glue meant for velvet. The beard itches like mad, but what is that compared with someone having nails hammered straight through their hands and feet?

Martin hears his mother calling. The sound of her voice cuts through the incessant abuse of the Pharisees, with their Jews' robes, turbans and frizzy beards. He must go and have his shower before Gran arrives. You never know, perhaps Gran will bring gingerbread with little bits of crystallized fruit in it. Jesus, the reindeer, slobbers. But he's not allowed to give in to the delicious, sweet, deadly sin of greed. Gran will have to go to purgatory on that count alone when she dies one of these days, because she forces him into a corner with that melting, cloyingly sweet temptation. Purgatory, where sinners wait unfed until the reindeer decides whether they must burn until the end of eternity or whether they'll be raised up to the highest clouds, where Jesus sits and laughs and says, 'Come in, we've been expecting you, my Father and I.'

The cross threatens to slide off his sweating shoulders. Mainly because he has to do his best not to step on any beetle or caterpillar or ant on his way to the mount of Goliath. That's why on TV Jesus staggered when he was right in the middle of a red sandy road. The only thing you are allowed to tread on, must tread on, if you ever come across it, is the snake that lived in the apple tree in paradise.

His mother shouts that she is going to fetch her mother from the station.

'OK!' Martin screams back.

'Get under the shower!'

No, Mum, atonement always come first. Mum shouts again. The rubber band round his forehead, stuck with sprigs of plastic holly, presses even harder. At one point Jesus was assisted by a simple bystander in dusty work-clothes. There are no bystanders here, because this is a district that Jesus has not yet passed by, Dad said. How surprised Dad would be if he came driving past in his Porsche and saw the son of God in the shape of his own child walking in his orchard! Martin scans the thin clouds. His other father, the one in heaven with his white beard, is nowhere to be seen either, although he is nevertheless expected to appear between the clouds to encourage his son. Like the team manager in the Tour de France, driving his convertible and calling out how many miles still to go to the lead rider, who is suffering in the French mountains. The heavenly father can pluck his son from the cross after his tortuous death and raise him up into heaven, and everyone will be taken by surprise. Martin suffers further difficulties; his legs fail him. Can he get the heretic Richard to come down off his thatched roof to help him? No, the man just sips that delicious, brain-numbing drink from his tin flask. (While all I'll get is a sponge full of vinegar shoved in my face, dammit.)

Would it be a deadly sin if he were to give up his solo journey to Goliath right now, end it here? You can undo a deadly sin. You tiptoe into a wooden cubicle with one wall full of holes, you confess your deadly sin, the priest listens and takes the deadly sin on to his own shoulders. Then he calculates how many kilos of sin you must atone for. There is a tariff: the weight of the sin is equal to such and such a weight of prayers, and that's it. He wipes the slate clean, and then no one is allowed to start nagging you about things that are over and done with.

But Martin isn't allowed to go inside the village church to investigate the confessional close up, though the boys at school and Miss Dora have talked about it, because his father, his former earthly father (who gave him a surname, put money in the bank for later when he'll be eighteen years old, and then disappeared) was a free thinker and turned Mum into a free thinker too. And that is awful, dreadfully shaming, because it means that they don't think anything, nor do they believe in anything at all. So it's no surprise that Jesus has no time for them and after they die he will send them straight to hell where they will burn, day in and day out, night in and night out, in one unending third-degree burn, from the infernal sun under the earth's crust.

Martin suffers, sweats, his whole body itches now, but he is not suffering enough. The Jews kick his ankles, the Romans punch his head and knees. Achilles the postman in his Pharisee's costume throws handfuls of sand in his mouth. Headmaster Goossens, as invisible as the other tormentors, although he is actually right there, approaches him from the road in his spotless clothes and looks at him as he so often does in the playground, with intrusive friendliness, more awkward than scornful, and says, 'So, Martin, everything OK?'

Martin hears himself answer, 'Yes, Headmaster.' And that is one of the worst heresies, because there is only one master in heaven and on earth.

'I'm thirsty,' Martin cries. No one comes to help him. Not even the person who was on the terrace just now in her bikini. Of course not: her mother comes before her son, who will cleanse and purify the sins of all mankind. Sheep approach him and nibble at his wet shirt.

'Fanta!' cries Martin. 'Cola, Fanta!' he calls to heaven.

Headmaster Willy Goossens's wife, Liliane, won't allow him to watch the bowling finals on BBC2 because her little darling has already worn his eyes out more than enough today correcting homework, and on Saturdays her Willy is hers entirely. True or not, my little spring chicken? Liliane, a grown-up woman of thirty-four, thoroughly gets on Headmaster Willy Goossens's nerves when she is so juvenile, but he did marry her for love and that carries responsibilities. In any case she has his interests at heart, as when she sees to it that he doesn't eat too many carbohydrates and fats, or when she brushes dandruff off his collar.

Headmaster Goossens listens to the third programme

because it is often very educational. One day, though it may be in the distant future, the third programme will broadcast what is now a typescript on the oak desk in front of him, his opus 1, a folder with thirty-six quarto pages in it. The purple-edged label on the folder bears his name in slanting letters, beneath the title in capitals: CYBELE. Underneath that is a line, and below that: *Rhapsody*, underlined. Thirty-six pages. All winter long he has toiled, evening after evening. While Liliane watched TV he scratched and scraped until that joyful moment in May when he laid down his fountain pen and whispered aloud to himself: 'Finished! I can do no better.' Liliane read it and said, 'It is deep, my little quail, darling, very deep, strange.' He explained the deeper meanings to her, the references, the citations, the structure, sometimes consulting a pocket dictionary. 'It's magnificent, my dearie, like everything you've written, but it's far too deep for me.'

So he had rewritten it completely. He tried to find a way to get every sentence across to her shabby, dull drain, and a month later he was ready with the final version. He did not read that out to her; he had already done so in his imagination, all those evenings. Sometimes he asked himself whether he really had even a smattering of talent, if what he did had to be so difficult, so short-sighted, cramped and hopeless. But then he thought of Flaubert and of Jeroen Brouwers who were quite satisfied with three or four lines a day. And they were famous writers, who worked at it the whole time, whereas he was in charge of the local school, the local history society, doing the regional reports for *The Morning*, arranging the Culture Weekened activities, and for his family, Liliane and their son Corry, the apple of their eye.

Goossens weighed the typescript in his hands. He was certain that the alderman in charge of cultural affairs would be pleasantly surprised by the weight when he was presented with *Cybele*. 'Why Goossens, you're on time with it. We're not used to that with artists.'

'I may not have much talent, sir, but I do stick to my obligations.'

'I shall certainly try to read it this coming week, but you know, this week we've got the debate on the tenders for our municipal library.'

'Of course, sir.'

'Cybele, Cybele, it escapes me just at the moment . . . something from antiquity, isn't it?'

'The goddess of fertility.'

'Quite so, precisely.'

'I have kept it fairly light, sir, bearing our people in mind, you see. In case it goes over their heads, if you see what I mean?'

'Congratulations, Goossens, right on time.'

The alderman had pronounced the title with a k. It would have been awkward to correct him. So be it: Kybele it is. Only eccentrics, maniacs, the obsessed would say Sybele as that s-sound has certain emotional overtones for them. Headmaster Goossens smiles. He hears Liliane busy in the kitchen. He takes a quick look at the TV guide. Perhaps he'll just watch the recorded showing of the Tour de France Gap-Briançon stage this evening. Generally the *Cybele* rehearsal gets into its stride a bit later on. 'Tempo, tempo, ladies!' Or perhaps he should interrupt the rehearsal, drawing a weary hand across his brow, and say, 'Boys, I can't go on any more, I'm sorry, I'm overworked.' But that would get back to the alderman at the town hall of course. 'Goossens is on his last legs.' 'Goossens has Aids.' No, he'll just have to get angry. His unbridled search for perfection will gain the upper hand, will dominate him. He'll throw his score at the wall, slam the door, boom 'Amateurs!' at them and hurry to his car. He'll be home at quarter past eleven. Liliane will have retired already, he can put the sports programme on with the sound down, lean back, Pale Ale in hand. But he's not allowed to shout 'amateurs' at them because they don't aspire to be anything more than unpaid volunteers who give up their free evenings for art. So what can he cry? 'Simpletons'?

The third programme is playing Beethoven, a trio. How pleasant, how soothing.

Liliane comes in and asks if he wants nuts in the salad this evening.

'Nuts?'

'It says so in *Marie-Claire*.'

'Which kind of nuts?'

'Walnuts.'

'There aren't any walnuts at the moment.'

'Out of a packet, silly!'

'Do what suits you best, Liliane.'

From time to time Headmaster Goossens says to his colleagues, 'I am thankful that I have Liliane.'

Liliane asks whether she should prepare a spinach omelette this evening. It's light, there's iron in spinach, and iron is good for the memory, and her little man needs his memory if he's got to rehearse this evening. She turns the radio off. 'That music is so depressing, don't you think? Or do you want to listen to it? Shall I put it back on?'

'Leave it,' says Headmaster Goossens.

'Then I'll let you get on with your work.' But she stands there. 'Kiss,' she says.

Headmaster Goossens kisses.

When they decided to build the house, he wanted his study to be next to the veranda. But Liliane said, 'Oh no, then you'll shut yourself away in there for hours and hours and I won't see you. Oh no, I can't be without you for so long, my heart. Ever since I was a little girl I've hated locked doors.'

Which is why he now sits at his small oak desk in an annexe of the living-room, separated from the living-room and kitchen by a half wall. The smell of soup and eggs drifts over, reflected off the ceiling, on to his hair and his papers.

36

Her sudden squawks when she's knitting and drops a stitch or when she knocks into things, and her burps and farts, penetrate into his delicate, enigmatic, creative thoughts, out of which *Cybele* has flowed as the tangible result.

Beethoven is the greatest of us all; he conquers pain.

Sometimes Headmaster Goossens feels a dejection that he cannot get to grips with, as though he is in the wrong body, finds himself in a wrong world, has to stray into a hostile age.

The last time this came over him was when he saw his own son Corry chatting with Martin Ghyselen, who was standing by the playground fence waiting for his mother. The contrast between the two boys of the same age pained him. Corry begins to look even more like Liliane's brother Johan, the same snub nose, that protruding lower lip, the blemished skin. Martin is beauty itself.

Innocent Corry is frightened of the dark, of thunderstorms, of all dogs (though his father would love to have a faithful Belgian sheepdog, which would jump up to him on winter evenings with its wet nose, and would lay its gently panting head in his lap). Corry hung on Martin's words while Martin expounded some argument or other, hands in his pockets, self-assured, self-satisfied like his mother. Headmaster Goossens walked over to the fence and said nonchalantly, 'Corry, Mummy is expecting you', and 'Everything OK, Martin?' and put his hand on Martin's warm, boyish neck; the long clammy hair fell on to his fingers.

'Yes, sir,' said Martin, looking over at the noisy older boys playing volleyball.

'Sir'. Not 'Headmaster', as the other boys would say. And then without a word or a gesture he had run across to Miss Dora, who appeared out from behind the volleyballers. 'The pain of jealousy is as a biting winter wind' says the fourth line of page fourteen of *Cybele*. And what is that strange relationship between Martin and Miss Dora about anyway?

37

They're always whispering together somewhere. He does not begrudge her that. The creature is loony. Because she's un-married. Said to be political. If it were up to him, he'd boot her out of his school, back to the convent school where she belongs. It is at such moments of demoralized pain that Headmaster Goossens would like to order Martin to have his hair cut. He could do so in line with specific ministry regulations. But it's not on. Never. It would be like hacking the nose off a marble kouros. Martin's mother would never stand for it anyway. Quite rightly.

According to Liliane, Martin's mother hasn't had a single lover since her husband walked out on her. Women know about each other like that. Women are wonders. Liliane as well as Sibylle, each at her own level.

He has invited Sibylle to the Culture Weekend. Not in his own name, naturally, but on behalf of the Culture Committee. Unsuspecting, haughty, conceited, she will sit in the third row, in seat number twenty-four, and as the *Rhapsody* unfolds, the lady will get goose-pimples, will press her thighs against each other, stare hungrily at the wings where she thinks that the perpetrator of this merciless portrayal of herself is hiding. Then, like a wild rabbit in a field caught in the car's headlights, she will stare at the Cybele in the footlights, and admit: 'The author of this scandalous performance knows me, has dissected me, idolizes me, throws himself at my feet, between my thighs.' The eunuchs' chorus, which makes the members of Concordia roar with laughter after so many rehearsals, will cause her to smile. The nymphs' chorus will penetrate her to her very core. Headmaster Goossens recites it silently to his bookcase:

O thou who reigns o'er beasts
of wood and land,
O thou who gladdens my eye,
my heart, my hand!

Unashamedly coarse rhymes, yes indeed. And Bruno Geerts from *The Evening News* will turn up his nose at them because the lout doesn't know that Goethe didn't find such rhymes beneath him for his *Faust*. But she, she who has inspired this, shall recognize it, for who else around her lives in an orchard close to the Zavelgem woods? Which other goddess has sheep and guinea fowl?

She who is secretly beloved,
and roams on the hills with her only child.

It is all on page three, how can it escape her?

She must already have sensed his adoration, although there hasn't been any visible sign. Or has there? The last time they met, in Rick the baker's, she was carrying two loaves under her arm. 'Hallo, Headmaster,' she said, and pushed past him. 'Headmaster.' ('I acknowledge you as my demanding, almighty and yet abject master.')

That afternoon during the maths lesson he had written out the penultimate pages of *Cybele*, rhymes and all.

But he still suffers pain. The pain of anticipation. Because *Cybele* is bound to be booed. It can't turn out any other way. People will never accept that a village school headmaster has any capacity for vision. They will think it an old-fashioned vision. His colleagues will smirk, particularly the gym teacher, who carries arrogant placards in the May Day procession. It will be the foul, incomprehensible bit of the Culture Weekend, while all the rest will be in line with the Minister's motto: the cultures of eating, fashion and leisure shall reign supreme. Liliane sympathizes. She said, 'Little bear, I'd rather not go with you to St Servatius, since I'll only tremble with nerves. I know that all the great minds were booed in their day, but you mustn't ask me to be there.'

Or should he hand out a duplicated sheet before the performance with an explanation? After all, ultimately, the ordinary spectator is being asked to swallow and digest in an hour and a quarter what has taken him months, months of study and musings with the help of mythological encyclopaedias and references. Headmaster Goossens scribbles angrily on a ministry envelope: 'The will, in greatest pain, brings forth ecstasy that emanates from itself, an ecstasy identical to that of pure intuition.' If they don't get that, they never will!

Liliane comes in. She cuddles up to him. 'Willy, I don't know what's up with me. I'm so restless. Willy, shouldn't the little bird visit the little mouse sometimes?'

'All right, right away,' says Headmaster Goossens. 'In ten minutes. I've still got some notes to make.'

Martin hides from Richard and the approaching BMW. Gran struggles out of the car, leaning on Mum's shoulder, wearing a ridiculous vanilla-coloured straw hat. He ought to run over to her and hug her now, but won't Richard laugh at him from his roof, won't he tease him about it later? Richard has been singing for the last hour, a sure sign that he is already well into the deadly sin of drunkenness. It would be brilliant if Richard and his gin flask crashed down off the roof right in front of the car tires, and why not right on top of Gran? It would take a miracle. But you're not allowed to pray for that kind of miracle.

There's a basket swinging on Gran's arm, probably

with their supper inside. She buys things cheaply just before the shops close in Antwerp, the largest port in the world. There won't be any sweets, because as a child Gran never had a single sweet from her backward parents. You never know though. Perhaps the shops still had some gingerbread left yesterday before they closed. 'Gran, Gran!' Martin cries, hurtling towards her.

'Boy, how grubby you are,' she says.

'He's playing at being an old man,' says Mum.

Martin grabs the last bits of wool from his cheeks.

'I've been in the shower.'

'That's good,' says Mum.

Gran has Mum's mouth and cheekbones. Her ravaged face is covered in a layer of powder, white ash in every wrinkle. Mum is going the same way, there's no escaping it. He takes the basket and swings it back and forth. 'Careful,' shrieks Gran, as though he would drop everything like she does. She doesn't even glance at Richard, but in the living-room she says, 'Sibylle, how can you have that boozer around the place?'

'Oh, he gets on with his work perfectly well.'

'But he's not an expert. You have to pay an expert more, but you don't get any nasty surprises afterwards.'

Gran's left eyelid trembles from time to time. Like a butterfly.

'Richard knows all about animals,' says Martin. 'Animals from the jungle and the desert. At the university he once had to cut open a kangaroo.'

'A kangaroo,' says Gran and goes to sit in Dad's chair, supporting herself on the dining table.

'Richard never lies. Has he ever lied, Mum?'

'Don't shout so, Martin.'

'But was he a vet or not?'

'Perhaps,' says Mum, anxious and cowardly like all women.

'I'd like to see that diploma of his,' says Gran, taking plastic bags out of her basket.

'I'll ask him. But maybe he's lost his diploma. He loses everything. Even his identity card,' says Martin. He tries to imitate Richard. The peevish laugh, rough voice, merry, defiant tone: 'And that suits me because I can't go on the dole.'

Gran takes a cardboard box with a picture of a pancake on it out of a plastic bag. 'Martin, he's not allowed to go on the dole. People like him can't vote either.'

'He's forfeited his civil rights,' Mum explains. 'That means you're not allowed to vote any more.'

'And a good thing too, otherwise he'd vote for the communists,' says Gran. She cuts through the cellophane over the box with a knife and carefully takes out thin dry wafers, pale with light brown spots.

'Hmmm. Matzos. It's been ages.' Mum says it in such a pleased, girlish voice that Martin looks up. Her face is usually annoyed and bored when Gran is there. And she doesn't say much either. But Gran doesn't notice because she's busy with her own confused squawking. But you can't blame Gran for that; she's alone for whole days at a time in her room in the port. She thinks most people are un-in-ter-es-ting.

The cakes look as if they haven't been in the oven long enough. Mum spreads butter on one and sprinkles brown sugar on top. Martin drools, tries, tastes, chews. The deadly sin of greed. Scrumptious. Is deadly sin always completely deadly sin? Rage, for example? A serious sin which he knows all about because a couple of hours ago he was still pretty angry. He threw his cross down on the grass with a curse and a dreadful crash when Mum called for the sixth time that he had to have his shower and interrupt his ascent to the mountain of Goliath. Jesus is no stranger to anger either. In the book he got from Miss Dora, *Jesus, the man*, which no one must see, it says that Jesus was angered by the tax collectors who plagued his father's house. He must check with Miss Dora that plaguing doesn't mean playing in the playground.

Gran slaps his hand with a serviette. 'Enough for today, that's already your fourth.'

'Mother, let him be.'

'All that butter and sugar, Sibylle! He must learn to control himself. He can't always have his own way.' Her left eyelid trembles; one day it will fly away like a butterfly. Then that eye will have to stay open all night, staring in the dark.

'How many times,' says Gran, starting off on one of her usual grumbles about the past, 'did Daddy tell you that you had no discipline at all, Sibylle, and that you'd pay for it one day?'

'Daddy was senile,' say Mum. In one corner of her unpainted his – for why does she have to put make-up on just for her mother? – there's a tiny splinter of sugar that Martin wants to lick away.

'A little respect,' says Gran, gathering the cake crumbs in her hands and dropping them into the ashtray. The ashtray has been there since Dad's time. Achilles the postman sometimes leaves a sodden cigarette butt in it if he has to wait while Mum signs for the letter with money from Dad, who won't pay Mum's monthly allowance into her bank because it would set a *president*. Mum, that angele on earth, hands Martin half of her wafer as she starts clearing away. He chews it slowly, making a delicious mush in his mouth, which he mixes with chocolate milk. Watch where Mum puts the wafers away. But she leaves the box where it is because Richard has turned up on the terrace. The sun splashes dozens of phosphorescent colours through the stained-glass window. Richard leans on the door frame and mumbles that he has no more wire, that Mum must fetch some more from town. Then he sees Gran.

'Look who's here now! It's been a long time, eh, Madam?'

'Not long enough,' says Gran, unbelievably rude.

'The thing is, time doesn't stand still, eh, Madam?'
Richard exaggerates, imitating a drunken man in a café. He
leans against the brick wall. Gran casts accusing, frowning
looks at Mum.

'The thing is, I don't have any more wire, but it doesn't
matter, there's plenty else to do, the glass, the grass. Hey,
Martin, where's your cross?'

'In the garden, near the tomatoes.'

'Richard, get on with your work now,' snaps Gran.

'The thing is, I . . . er . . . that is . . .' Martin recognizes
the absent-mindedness, the mental block; it is the drinker's
punishment. He helps out. ' . . . that you haven't got any
more wire.'

'Exactly, Martin. Exactly.' Richard falls full length on
to the black stone floor without putting his arms out in front
of him. He raises himself up on an elbow and waves to Martin.
Then he crawls back to the terrace on his hands and knees.
They hear him singing an army song.

'And you can laugh?' Gran is talking to Mum, not
him. Mum is smiling warmly in the direction of the orchard.

'Should I cry?'

'Do you consider this is behaviour that . . .'

'Behaviour, behaviour. That man gets up every day in
a good mood, gets on with his work, and falls into his bed
drunk at night. What more do you want?'

'A fine example for Martin!'

'I'll never drink a drop. Never ever in my whole life.'

'That's good, Martin,' says Mum, but she doesn't
mean it.

'He'll be back in prison again, mark my words. And
then you two'll say: Gran told us so.'

'Has Richard already been in prison, Mum?'

She shrugs her shoulders, stacking plates. She abandons
her child. She is the old woman's daughter.

'Mum. I'm asking you something . . .'

'Martin, stop that shrieking.'

'Why was he in prison? Did he kill somebody?'

'Another time, Martin.'

'No! Now!' She won't answer because the old woman is there. She doesn't want it to look as though she always lets him have his way.

'OK,' says Martin. 'Tell me about it another time. But then can I have one more mats?'

She butters another, avoids the old woman's reprimanding look, mixes brown sugar into the butter, wipes her fingers.

Martin grabs the wafer too eagerly, it breaks down the middle, but he rescues both halves. Water pours from behind his tongue. He bites.

'Not *mats*,' says Gran. '*Matzo*. It means unleavened bread.'

'Passover bread,' says Mum.

'The Jews' bread. They eat this, not bread like we do.'

An acidic cramp shoots into his stomach full of chocolate milk. The two sins, anger and greed, burn in his belly. There is buzzing and hammering inside his skull. He can't hold it back: his lips are torn open by iron claws and a yellow-brown wave crashes onto the tablecloth, the plates, Gran's dress. 'It's the Jews,' he says, and the salty scorching invades his nostrils, the back of his throat, his eyes. The two women who were about to poison him with that Jewish food have jumped to their feet. Mum tries to catch hold of him but he pushes her arm shiny with suntan oil aside. He points a knife at Gran's left eye. 'You two are in league with the Jews! Behind my back!'

'Which Jews?'

Once again, once again Mum is playing the innocent. Oh how deeply she is implicated! Her face twisting, the rickety old woman emits a stifled scream. Her daughter raises a threatening hand with mother-of-pearl fingernails.

'Sibylle,' says Gran, 'what in God's name have you told that boy?'

'Which Jews, Martin?'

He stumbles over his words. 'Those filthy ones, stinkers, with their beards, who never wash themselves. . . .'

Mum takes hold of his T-shirt and squeezes his chin. 'Who said that?'

'Everybody knows it.'

'Who's everybody?' She is hurting him, her nails are digging into his cheek.

'It was on TV two weeks ago.'

'What was on TV?'

'The film about Jesus. Look in the TV guide.'

'That stupid film.' She lets go of him.

'Did the Jews kill Jesus or not?'

A dead straight wrinkle appears between her eyebrows, her thought-wrinkle, her free-thinking wrinkle, as she tries to remember.

(He: 'Can I watch that film, Mum? Go on, please?' She, from her bed: 'But no later than ten o' clock.' And he watches until at least until half paste ten of course, setting the sin of disobedience against the crescendoing, breathtaking climax when the reindeer moaned on that bloody mountain and asked his father why he had forsaken him, and then hung between the two villains, the good and the bad one, who looked like a small version of Sylvester Stallone.)

Mum becomes ugly from the effort of remembering. 'So that's why you've been so difficult all that time and why you're walking about playing Calvary with a cross.' She turns to her mother, to give her due acknowledgement. Your mother is with you for the whole of your life. 'I thought it would pass, would pass by itself.'

'You see, Sibylle,' says Gran, who never sees anything.

Martin has to help his mother wipe up the vomit. Gran goes to collect up Mum's returnable bottles from the kitchen and store room, which she will take in to get the deposit money.

'They don't show on TV that the Jews don't wash themselves,' says Mum. 'Who told you such things? Martin, answer me!'

'Stupid ass,' calls Gran. 'Just like his father.'

'Mother, leave Gerard out of this.'

'You don't want to hear the truth.'

'Martin, answer me or I'll . . .'

'Or I'll? Or I'll what?'

'Or I'll box your ears.'

'Do it. Go on. I beg you. Go on.' Did Jesus get a beating from his mother? It doesn't say so in *Jesus, the man*. Nine out of ten not. On the contrary, she took him to her heart. And at the end she stood on the left by the cross, her tearful face level with his injured knees.

'Or has Irene been telling you that twaddle?'

Martin bursts out laughing. Irene, who can't count to ten, who has married a shrimp fisher.

'Jews are people too,' says Gran, out of breath from putting her bottles by the front door.

'Or do the boys at school invent these things?'

'Invent! That bunch stabbed Jesus through his heart, gave him vinegar to drink, made holes in his hands and feet with nails.' His voice cracks. 'But they didn't finish him off, those rotters, because he rose after three days!'

'Then evidently he could cope with it,' says Gran. At that moment Martin wants to hit her over the head with one of her bottles.

'Martin, don't be so hysterical. Martin, listen. Are you listening?'

'Yes.'

'Yes who?'

'Yes, Mum.'

'Jesus really was a Jew.'

48

'What? Never in his life!'

'Born of a Jewish mother as far as I'm aware.'

'Quite logical,' says the old woman by the front door.

'Ha ha ha,' says Martin. It sounds weak.

'Martin, what was Jesus, according to you?'

'Not a Jew.'

'What then?'

'A Catholic.' It sounds false as he says it out loud. (Verily, verily I say unto you, said the reindeer. But what did he say next? He never said he was a Catholic.)

Martin screams, 'You mustn't have anything to do with Jewish food. If you see a Jew you must make the sign of the cross and walk on the other side of the road.'

'Martin, don't be so hysterical!'

'You can talk!'

'Martin, if you don't tell me right now who you've picked this nonsense up from, you'll go to the rabbit shed immediately and stay there until later this evening. Perhaps all night.'

Martin is not allowed to tell the truth. He has sworn on the head of this same person who is pursuing him so furiously that he will never reveal who has converted him to the only true faith. If he were to tell the truth, a saintly dying woman would be martyred during the last days of her life by being turned out on the street in front of her house, by losing her job on account of the guilt of people like Dad and Gran and Mum and Mr Goossens, who are free thinkers and who mock the reindeer cruelly and are not a jot better than those Pharisees and tax collectors.

'You've got ten seconds,' says Mum.

Martin looks at her wrist-watch and precisely nine seconds later says: 'Mr Goossens.'

(Not: Headmaster Goossens. There is only one master, who is nicknamed Rabbi.)

'Mr Goossens? I don't believe it. When?'

49

'In the lesson about foreign people, their traditions and customs.'

'You got a six in geography. You must have misunderstood,' says Gran, who can't remember a single name, only numbers.

'Go to your room, Martin,' Mum snaps. In the bathroom he gulps down three glasses of water one after the other and gargles with the leftovers of Dad's aftershave, but he can't get the taste of the Jews out of his mouth.

Miss Dora cycles up the Kapellebos hill as never before. She has wings. Although the wind is balmy and weak, it seems to be pushing her forwards from behind. She breathes in and out with deliberate breaths. She doesn't want to die before Christmas, she won't. It would be too unfair. She still has to finish training Excelsior, her women's choir, for the performance on Christmas Eve. Her music lessons at the College of Our Lady in town and at the village school in Zavelgem are duties that she undertakes with love, but the Excelsior choir is her life's work. Apart from the salvation of Martin Ghyselen of course, which is of another order, a rare manifestation of mercy.

The priest at Zavelgem asked her to have her choir sing at the Culture Weekend to counteract the influence of the liberals, who have no real connection with St Servatius; the church has already been deconsecrated and is rented out to the town authorities.

'A couple of altos still need polishing,' she replied.

'Polish them then,' he growled. Miss Dora has resolved to stay alive until Christmas, until she can take out her Christmas Nativity scene with its figures wrapped up in brown paper, and set it up in her living-room.

She reaches the top of the hill out of breath and gets off her bicycle. Perhaps she will still be able to see the view by the time it is covered in snow, the farms, factories and woods. In a nearby meadow, children are playing with a kite, they throw paper butterflies after the billowing, swaying dragon, messages to heaven.

It may not be seemly behaviour for a teacher, but Miss Dora nevertheless sits down on the verge beside the road. In fact she feels like having a little nap now, in the dry grass. She dozes off and then opens her eyes wide. She must dedicate every moment that she is prey to that tangle of eager worms in her body to the Redeemer.

Now. She thinks of her Martin. How sweetly it began.

She was walking along the corridor between the school buildings and heard the cigar-laden voice of the priest going on about Absalom – rather appropriate at a time when Arabs and Jews want to kill each other. It sounded stuffy. Not that she would ever dare to comment (at least not in public) on the way he teaches religion. After all, talent is, like a full singing voice, unevenly distributed on earth. But she found his uninspired, perfunctory drone worthless.

At that moment, on that grey day, in that dark school corridor, where thin sunlight absorbed by watery wisps of cloud was the only light through the window, she was on her way to the third form to practise 'Finestra che lucevi', when she heard the voice. It was not a natural voice. It did not come out of a larynx, not from inhaling and exhaling. It was rather her own inextinguishable longing for a voice, which turned into vibrations belonging more inside herself than in the pale air that surrounded her. The voice said 'Now!', in the silence of that moment, like a slap in her face. 'Now', in a flash, the duration of the imperceptible sound. At that instant she saw Martin Ghyselen standing in an odd, twisted position with his cheek against the door of classroom B5. He had pushed his long hair back so that he could press his ear closer to the door. Afterwards she also realized he was standing on top of his Nikes.

'What are you doing here, Martin?'

He wasn't frightened. He moved away from the door, with that stubborn tic she recognized from when he once got bad marks in her music lesson.

'Waiting,' he said, and walked away past the window through which you could see the empty playground with the board saying 'Long Live Flanders!'

'What are you waiting for?'

'Until the priest has finished.'

She caught up with him just as he got to Headmaster Goossens's classroom and touched his sleeve. Headmaster Goossens was droning a multiplication table. Afterwards, it seemed to her that she had snatched the boy from the heathen's path between two mighty sources of sound, each cancelling the other out, the bass of the priest that blared on about Absalom, and the nervous Heldentenor (no higher than B flat) of someone who found his faith in so-called exact ideas.

'What were you doing there in the corridor, Martin?'

'Listening,' the boy said sullenly.

He was not allowed to be there on his own; it was against the rules. The official consequences could be nasty.

'But aren't you meant to be studying with Mrs Sorgheloos?'

'She's got a cold. At least that's what she said.'

'Was she here?'

'She got a message to Headmaster Goossens.'

Miss Dora had always thought it absurd that an ethics teacher had been specially recruited for one pupil with atheist parents who forbade him from attending religious instruction lessons. This exposed him to the distrust and scorn of his fellow pupils; he might possibly be branded for the rest of his life. Miss Dora respected other people's convictions – morals and rationality in themselves couldn't do all that much harm – but this was too crazy for words. Particularly as Mrs Sorgheloos is separated, and often doesn't turn up, doubtless encouraged, or at any rate not reprimanded by the headmaster.

'Now.'

She still held the sleeve of his denim jacket between her fingers. She waited for the voice and caught it again through her own hurried, inarticulate inner thoughts: Dora, your moment has come, the moment of illness, of deadly growths in your body, the moment of a single duty, the moment for one soul and that soul is the soul of the boy with the wild hair, innocent as one of the little shepherds in the Nativity scene, beset with doubts from all around.

'Why were you listening at that door?'

'Because the priest tells stories so beautifully.'

'Do you think so?'

Almost every day for the next few weeks she had read aloud to him hurriedly from her New Testament, the two of them together in the afternoons in the school dining-room. She had told him her secret, how she would soon be turned into shreds of lifeless tissue which would be gathered up into purgatory in the world of shadows. She had implored him not to tell anyone who had initiated him into the truth, the

way and the life. Because as ever, as in the time of the cata-
combs, true Christians, the poor and the innocents would be
pursued by liberals, socialists and all present-day heathens in
the establishment.

As the weeks passed, Miss Dora noted with pride and
gratitude that she was able to sing higher and more strongly
in lessons. She and Martin exchanged burning looks. She
gave him the book by Canon Versijp that dealt with Jesus as
a man. Oh, may this 'Now' last until Christmas.

Miss Dora climbed back on to her bicycle. She would
slow down as she passed the Ghyselens' country house. 'I
seem well loved. Better late than never,' she said, giggling,
and rang her bicycle bell vigorously.

The police commissioner stood with his legs apart in the cell smelling of disinfectant and Clara's perfume, and listened to Clara's complaints. She kept wanting to fall on his neck; each time he moved her away kindly.

'But how can I look after my cats if I can't look after my clients, Mr Commissioner?'

'It's not allowed, Clara.'

'And those girls along Veurnesesteenweg, with their naked bottoms in the window? That's allowed. Especially when my clients are neat, distinguished citizens, mature, blameless.'

'It's not allowed, Clara.'

'But there's so much that's not allowed!' cried that ancient, loyal face, sallow and bony.

'It's the law, Clara.'

On the way back to the security of his office he was buttonholed by a group in Sunday clothes, Jehovah's Witnesses. They wanted to convert him; he walked on. Then he hurried, thinking it was unwise to leave Lippens alone with Richard Robion for too long.

He detected it immediately from Lippens's jovial, relaxed stance. The damage had been done. Lippens had hit the man in the face, although it was against every rule, against all common sense. The man stood in a vaguely military position by the desk, holding the small of his back and shivering. His cheek was red and swollen. The police commissioner sent Lippens out to the snack bar for six cheese rolls. He pushed the man by the shoulder until he sat down.

They faced each other in silence. The only sound was that squelching when the man shifted his shoes. Opposite the police station a house was being demolished. The pockmarked concrete blocks, the framework of loose planks, the dusty cables, shreds of wallpaper, a broken sofa, made the police commissioner feel dejected.

The house would be rebuilt again and pulled down again.

The man seemed to be thinking the same. A resigned expression came over his face, as though he too were suppressing some sorrow or other and was lost in calm contemplation. The police commissioner consulted his diary. On two pages it said: 'Culture Weekend. Lunch: Governor' in his cramped handwriting.

'That policeman knows his stuff,' said the man. 'He's hurt me badly.'

'He can't stand it if he's provoked. He's one of the old school.'

'Not like you, eh?'

'No.' The police commissioner thought, I do not want to go home at all. It is unreasonable, but I can't bear the decline and revival of things.

'How much longer do you think you'll stay in the police?'

'What's that to you?' said the police commissioner, surprised.

'Don't you have to retire?'

It made the hairs on his neck stand on end to realize that his decline was so obvious to this man, this wreck. 'Enough drivelling,' he sneered. 'Your wife . . .'

'No,' said the man loudly. 'Leave her in peace.'

'You should have left her in peace.'

The man struck the top of the desk with the flat of his hand. The bronze inkstand bounced.

'No, I say.'

'Very well.' Silence. Good thing Lippens wasn't witnessing this. Two men in Sunday suits were wandering about in the demolished house. They climbed over the concrete blocks. Pigeons fluttered by.

The miserable voice of Ronald Veydt, the journalist from *The People,* resounded in the corridor; he was probably asking Naessens why the criminal was being held for so long at the police station. Because it suits me, Veydt.

The man dropped the roll when Lippens held it out to him. He grabbed at it with an uncommonly large hand; he picked a triangle of cheese off his black and red spattered ankle, wiped his hand on his trousers.

'You can eat off the floor here,' said Lippens.

When the man had finished eating he began to talk. The police commissioner's irritation had rather ebbed away as he watched him eating, but it was stirred up again by the way he adopted the local peasants' way of speaking, hesitating, scattering everything with er's. He wasn't a peasant but he chose to use their surly stammering. It cast doubt on every unfaltering sentence, making it seem suspicious, slippery urban deception.

'I had to. I had to get down off the roof at one point. My flask was empty. You know how it is when a flask is empty. Dead drunk? No. But I was horizontal more than I was vertical on the roof. Miss Dora came by, the music teacher. On her bicycle. I thought, she's heading for trouble. Seeing her situation. That's what they say. Oh, they talk such a lot. She went by again later on. But by then I had already passed out in the tomatoes.'

I must make a note, thought the police commissioner, and let notary Dockx have this for his local dialect dictionary. 'Pass out in the tomatoes': to collapse unconscious, from excessive consumption of alcohol.

Habit made him continue listening to the lies, the broken sentences, the senseless digressions, because fragments of police truth could be gleaned from them. But also because he wanted to keep the man in his room. I want to draw it out, delay, he realized, he noted, as though recording in his diary. Just as this one opposite me stammers and shuffles on the floor in his wet squeaking shoes and wants to postpone the memory of his stinking, foul deed with the flies swarming about at quarter to ten this morning. 18 Belsele Street. I shall not go home. Can I help it that I can't love her any more?

Meanwhile, without a pause the man said in a breathless grunt, 'You can see a long way from up there. If there's no mist in the Verdegem valley you can see the towers of Oudenaarde. And much else besides. Two blokes in camel-hair jackets in a stationary Lada for half an hour. A woman with a fat arse crying. The girls from the boarding school on their bicycles. Miss Dora.'

'You've already said that.'

'Denis from the greengrocer's too. In his 2CV. He comes to see where he can pinch apples from at night . . .'

The police commissioner interrupted him. 'Did you sometimes fancy the lady where you worked?'

'I? No. At my age.'

'Have you ever given her trouble?'

'Those years are over.'

'Forty-four. So you could still get your dick up,' said Lippens.

'Not in my case.'

'We're going to break you,' said Lippens.

'What is that lady's name where you work?'

'Ghyselen. I've already said that ten times.'

'And her first name?'

'Sibylle,' said the man.

'What?'

'Sibylle,' he repeated. His mouth fell open. He forgot to close it.

'Why are you blushing?'

'I am embarrassed on your behalf, Mr Commissioner.'

'Hey, now hold on a minute,' said Lippens.

The police commissioner is getting a headache, as though an invisible pair of spectacles has been placed on his nose, a steel frame squeezing his temples, his eye sockets. He used to be able to construct a systematic cross-examination out of such aimless drivel, gather proof, pull out headlines from the disorderly material of the crime, determine the profit and loss of an interrogation.

Lippens took over. The names of the cafés the man had visited after work. The Little Rose at Fernand. Rustica on the motorway. Margriet's. How long he had stayed, how he got home, how many kilometres from the Ghyselens' house to his house in the town. What else he had done at the Ghyselens' when Mrs Ghyselen had cycled off towards the village.

'I got hold of the little one. He kicked out and hit me but I managed to get him into the rabbit shed.'

The man rolled up his shirt sleeve, inspected the light blue worms swelling up on his underarm; he scratched them and laughed at Lippens.

'You've hurt me badly.'

'I warned you,' said Lippens. 'You've got to answer when I speak to you.'

'The little one,' said the man, leaning forwards to deliver a private confidential warning to the police commissioner. 'The little one kept on and on crazily with his tales about Jesus. Because he thinks he is Jesus himself. . . .'

The police commissioner saw that the man's beard had grown vigorously since he had been found that morning, babbling, blind, legs splayed out on the grained lino floor, gasping for breath. Beard growth through anxiety, through remorse.

'. . . on the mount of Goliath,' said the man.

'The mount of Golgotha.'

'The little one said Goliath.'

'Goliath, that's something else,' said the police commissioner gently.

Martin gouged the bark of a silver birch with a blunt table knife; it was difficult to loosen. He would have been better off snatching a potato peeler out of the drawer by the draining board, but he had yet to learn to be observant, like Clint Eastwood, even in the most consuming, absurd rage.

Gran shouted to him to keep away from the tree. Come off it! These are Dad's trees and Dad has definitely put it into his will that all the trees in the orchard – which he must count one of these days – will come to him, the only heir. Unless Dad makes a new heir with his new girl-friend. We'll see about that. All the same, watch out, half-brother, second person, here comes the swordfish.

Martin grasps the knife in his fist and holds it out in front of him. He leans forwards and cleaves through the Mediterranean Sea. He hoots and squeals, which isn't so foolish because fish make a hellish noise under water. He stalks his half-brother's pale shadow through the seaweed and caves. He turns away by the cherry trees and heads for Gran. The swordfish, feared by all sea creatures, will slice diagonally through that floral dress, spike the contents on its lance, flashing as though through a school of mackerel. He brakes, lets the lance drop. A low-flying fighter jet drowns his hooting.

'Martin, come here!'

'Why?'

'Because I say so.' That eternal reply.

You aren't my parent, only a grandparent, and they can't call their souls their own. Grandparents are nothing. Neither fish nor fowl. And in second place over all. Just as Jesus is the second person of the Trinity, placed second after his father who is number one in all circumstances.

Gran shuffles across the mossy brick steps of the terrace, walks past the rhododendron and leans on the ochre-painted wall. Dad and Mum had decided on the colour of the outside walls after their trip to Italy, where all walls are that colour. It was a very long time ago. It's pretty strange that he wasn't there then. Or perhaps he was already inside Mum's tummy. And his heart was already beating.

Gran continues shouting, this time in Richard's direction. She orders him to bring Martin to her immediately and, believe it or not, the wimp obeys. He creeps slowly but not unwillingly down the swaying ladder. A haze of bits of straw surrounds his silhouette.

Martin flees. He reaches the stout lime tree which is at least a hundred years old and therefore has survived many wars and which Dad called 'my tree'. He hears Gran ranting and raving, he sees Richard stoop to tie his shoelace, stand up and begin to run. Martin leaves the lime tree and bolts towards the hedge, then to the hole in the hedge where the weeds are as tall as a person and where the slugs, bats and rats live.

It doesn't take long for Richard to catch up with him, seize him, lift him triumphantly up into the air, his sour breath on Martin's face.

'Judas,' says Martin. Richard throws him over his shoulder with difficulty. Martin swings, hits, kicks, because that is expected of him, but though he continues to growl and wriggle, a cool calm comes over him. Then he lets his body go slack and be carried by this moving, calmly walking fence. As though he has used up today's ration of the deadly sin of anger.

'Richard, put me down,' he says and Richard responds to his composure.

'Thanks, Richard,' he says and puts his hand in the conqueror's, a rough wooden glove of a hand.

'Into the shed,' says Gran. 'Into the shed. Until your mother gets back.'

The animal smell from the rabbit shed is already noticeable by the cherry trees, and really bad at the door of Dad's billiard room, even though the rabbits have been dead for months. One morning they were all lying there with their white tummies up. They possess eternal life, which is why they still stink so long after they've died. The eternal life of all the dead who have stayed on the true path. Just as the cherry blossoms come back each year. Sinners have eternal life too, but in boiling oil in their case.

'And you went into the rabbit shed straight away with Richard?' asked Miss Dora four days later, three days after the horror.

'Yes. Straight away.'

'Because you felt your Gran was right?'

'Yes. You're not allowed to damage trees. It's as bad as clubbing baby seals to death. Trees can cry too, only we can't see it.'

65

'Good, Martin, very good. And what did Richard do with you in the rabbit shed?'

'Chat.'

'Only chat? He doesn't say much usually.'

'He does to me.'

'About what? Don't you want to tell me? You don't have to if you don't want to.'

Martin wanted to hug Miss Dora more than ever, protect her, comfort her, so grateful was he that he didn't have to betray Richard. Anyway, as soon as Miss Dora is dead and has arrived in that cloudless bright blue heaven, she'll be able to look out over everything from there, not only whatever is going on at that moment, but also everything that has happened during her life, a video that plays back absolutely everything. Three days and three nights after Richard's horrible deed, Martin asked himself whether Richard's wife Julia would bump into Miss Dora in heaven, by chance (as it was ninety-five per cent certain she would end up there).

Did the dead walk along together in the street there? Heaven is a pretty big place. Perhaps it gets crowded in the good spots, in Jesus's neighbourhood, where there are phosphorescent armchairs sculpted in the clouds.

'I would like to tell, Miss Dora, but I must ask Richard's permission first, and they won't let me in to the prison.'

'No,' said Miss Dora. 'Only immediate family.'

'But he hasn't got any family.'

'He that mischief hatches mischief catches,' said Miss Dora sternly, like a policeman.

'Come on,' says Richard and moves the rusty bolt aside. Martin goes into the bare shed. Only mouldy walls and some shrivelled carrots and wet straw are left on the ground where the nibblers used to be, where there used to be grazing, squeaking and scratching. The rustle of the spring flowing past the wall. Martin pushes thick spiders' webs out of the way; the door closes. The only light is from a small, dirty, wired-glass window. Then he notices that Richard has come inside the shed too and is leaning quietly against the wall, getting out his tobacco and rolling a cigarette.

'We're both in prison,' says Martin.

'It's not a prison if you can get out, if there's no keyhole.'

'Gran said when we were at the table that you had already been in prison once. Did my Mum know that?'

'I dare say.'

'And my Dad?'

'Him for sure.'

'And they let you loose at our place? I'd never want anyone about the house who'd been in prison.'

'Your parents are good people.' Richard takes a gulp from his flask.

'Let me have a drink.'

'Only a taste.'

The liquid scorches Martin's mouth; he only just manages to keep it in. It's fire. He sneezes three, four times.

'It's strong,' he gasps.

'The weakest. A brickie: for bricklayers, who can go on drinking it when the weather's freezing.'

'Does Julia drink this too?'

'No. Our Julia prefers cognac.'

'Does she drink as much as you?'

'Not more but not less either.' Richard laughs aloud, as though at a joke.

Martin had once met Julia at her house, a slum on the outskirts of the town. The three chairs and the unpainted table looked as though they had been dumped there. Julia's bare feet were resting on a cat lying on a broken sofa. The stove glowed; so did Julia. Her voice was too rough, too harsh for her delicate figure. 'Do you want some chocolate? Milk or plain?'

67

But she had eaten it herself that afternoon.

'She is so forgetful,' Richard said tenderly.

'That drunkard likes you,' she said. 'Much more than me.'

'I don't believe that,' said Martin. No, he said: 'I don't think so,' because she shouted immediately, 'Think, think, what do you know about thinking, booby? I go crazy thinking to myself the whole time. I have to take aspirins for it every day.'

'One aspirin has never done anyone any harm,' said Richard, unusually tender. He poured coffee from the pot on the stove and slurped it noisily.

'Martin,' said Julia, 'do you know that the whole time I've been with that wild ape, I've only ever been to the sea once? Once for three days, and in those three days he didn't even see the sea, he stayed in the lodgings all that time.'

'You could see the sea out of the window,' said Richard.

'And one day I went for a walk for an hour or so on the beach and when I came in he said, "Well, Julia, have you been thinking about me?" and I was shocked. I thought: He must be pretty pleased to see me if he can ask a thing like that, and I said, "Yes, Richard, I've been thinking about you because I think about you all the time when you're not with me." "Well," he says. I say, "Well what?" "Well, where's my pint?" His lordship thought I'd gone out to fetch his pint of beer. I'll drop dead if that isn't true.'

'How are things with Julia?' asks Martin in the rustling rabbit shed full of swarming flies.

'Very good.'

'But she drinks too much.'

'Julia is an orphan child,' says Richard sadly. 'And orphan children need more affection than others. When they don't get affection they drink too much.'

'Why were you in prison?'

The drunkard doesn't answer. Someone is shuffling in

68

the yard outside. Gran. Go away, you old female, now that the two of us are so cosy in here, like two naughty pupils standing in the corner and winking at each other. Martin picks up one of the dark brown shrivelled carrots and breaks it in two. The stink is unbearable. He had often teased the rabbits: they jumped up against the wire netting and at the last minute he pulled a carrot away from their busy, trembling noses.

'I was put away because I helped people.'

'They don't put anyone in prison for that.'

'They did me.' Richard takes a gulp and shivers as though in a sudden cold wind. 'I'm not saying you mustn't help people. I'm saying they can put you away pretty quick if you do.'

'Which people?'

'Women.'

'Which women?'

'Women who thought I could do something about their misery because I was a qualified person. Lokeren is a small town and those women didn't dare go to their usual doctor. It's a while ago, and the laws aren't so strict now, that's to say, they overlook things. But not then. When they'd been helped they asked me, "Richard, what do I owe you?" And when I said, "Nothing, but be a bit careful from now on," they said, "Oh, Richard, I'll never forget that!" But when the police came they were the first to point their fingers at me.'

'Is there a crucifix in your house?'

'Yes. Orphan children are brought up with it.'

'I mean in the house where you used to live, in Lokeren?'

'I don't believe so.'

'You see! If you'd prayed in front of the crucifix in time it would never have happened.'

Outside Gran is shouting like a lost, cross turkey.

'Children,' says Richard. 'Children. Why have them? Because you're frightened of crawling into your grave alone?'

Sunlight pours into the shed. Gran is standing in the

doorway in shadow, but you can see her hideous face clearly enough.

'What are you two doing here? Come out of there, Richard, out of there!'

Richard shuffles towards the light in a swirl of dust and flies, like a schoolboy told off by the head teacher.

'You too,' snarls Gran. Martin pushes past Richard's backside and sneaks out. He can hear Richard stammering something to the old woman.

Oh gods! Which merciful god has sent her? Headmaster Goossens sees Sibylle Ghyselen lean her bicycle against the bay of his house and tidy her dishevelled hair. He hurries to the front door before Liliane can answer the bell.

He can't think of a greeting. 'Yes, Madam,' he says, as though to a Jehovah's Witness. She asks if she can speak to him.

'Of course. Always.'

Liliane is less impressed than Headmaster Goossens expected. She leads Sibylle Ghyselen affably into the living room.

'Don't look at the mess,' he says. Everything he says

is unworthy. He adds, 'It's about Martin, I assume.'

'What an angel of a boy,' cries Liliane. 'We are delighted with him!' Uninvited, she sits down opposite Sibylle Ghyselen, her thick, proletarian legs sticking out. 'And to me that hair of his is so beautiful, especially when it has just been washed. Long hair doesn't suit everyone, but I think it looks lovely on him.'

'Mr Goossens, might I be able to speak to you alone?'

'Of course,' Liliane wails. 'I understand. I'm going right away.' She doesn't budge an inch. 'What about a cup of coffee? I've got decaffeinated, too. Or a biscuit? No? You, Willy? No? That's a first.'

Headmaster Goossens is ashamed. He sees his living-room through the eyes of the goddess Cybele: the copper candlesticks, the chandelier, the porcelain vases, the shoddy lamp on the window sill, the photo of Corry as a cub scout. Oh, why didn't she warn him of her visit, so that he could have taken her elbow and guided her straight into his office, where she would have discovered his true nature, his asceticism, the absence of clutter. His trace of irritation that she had turned up just like that without phoning or giving any warning – she wouldn't have dreamt of doing it to her entrepreneur husband's friends – is smothered by joy. She is here, even though it is in Liliane's territory of copper, floral prints and mahogany.

'If you need me, just call,' says Liliane, and leaves them alone.

Then Sibylle Ghyselen recounts a scandalous thing. An accusation so absurd that he can scarcely breathe as he says, 'You can't really mean that? How could I have anything against the Jews?' and 'I can't imagine where this accusation comes from' and 'I shall get to the bottom of it. This is dangerous. How could Martin accuse me of such a thing? I take great care that his rights are respected precisely because he is the only one not attending religious instruction lessons. When did he say this?'

'This afternoon.'

Through the window with its amber film of dried rain splashes, Headmaster Goossens sees Denis from the greengrocer driving past very slowly. He hopes Denis will load Sibylle's bicycle, the glittering evidence of her presence, into his van.

'If anyone regrets the agonizing schism between the Christians and the Jews, Madam, it is I. One could certainly argue about the recent behaviour of the State of Israel, but that doesn't mean that during lessons or at other times I would ever. . . .'

'My son,' she says.

'Your son,' he says, 'must have picked up the wrong idea from somewhere. He has many fantasies.' What he needs is a good hiding, that spoilt brat.

'And not from you?'

'Madam! How dare you suspect that I . . . the Jews and us . . . that tragic separation of enemy brothers . . . a continuing torment in history. . . .'

She is not listening, but she believes him.

'Well, who then?'

'Madam, I must ask you to keep this *entre nous*, but it wouldn't surprise me if the priest had something to do with this. Without fully realizing it of course. Possibly he puts things rather colourfully in his lessons. And then the pupils embroider on it in the playground.'

'Then I shall ask the priest about it.'

Headmaster Goossens sucks on a cold, empty pipe, puts it down with the bowl on the edge of the ashtray. A frown appears on Sibylle Ghyselen's forehead, almost like a scar. He doesn't want her to leave. He asks, 'Have you received an invitation to the Culture Weekend?'

'No.' She is lying. He himself typed the envelope with the Culture Committee logo. Her address made him tremble.

'Something of mine is being put on under the auspices of the Culture Weekend.'

'Where?'

'St Servatius.'

'Something of yours?' Will she pull his leg, mock?

He tells her about his *Rhapsody*. About the rehearsals.

'I have to make do with what I've got, of course. Our Concordia Society has outstanding people, but they have done farces and comedies in the main. This is a complete switch. And I've had to limit the number of roles. So I had to dispense with a choir of dwarves to represent Cybele's rituals. Now I have just one dwarf played by little Mariette Verhaegen.'

'Have you ever seen a frozen dwarf?'

'No,' he says, puzzled.

'I have. In Alaska, on a trip with my husband.'

'You've been to Alaska?'

'On the way to the United States. We had to make an emergency landing in Alaska and spend a night there. And in the morning, just in front of the hotel, there was a dwarf covered with icicles.'

The veiled lips allow the shadow of an ironic smile, signal a message intended for him alone. Headmaster Goossens wishes, as he so often does, but this time more painfully than ever, that he was ten centimetres taller, or at the least five, that he had broader shoulders, that he could hypnotize.

'Yes, nature is cruel sometimes,' he says.

Then she says she is glad to hear that besides his work as head teacher he still has the time and zest to devote himself to a hobby. A hobby! He gives a half smile.

I am cut to the quick. Why do they always put our passions into such painful perspective, goddesses like Cybele, women like Liliane?

She says that her husband didn't have any hobbies, which was a shame in her view. He was always at it with his various businesses, all kinds of responsibilities for schemes that demanded his energy all at once. Constantly on the plane to America, back and forth. Living a dozen lives at the same time.

Headmaster Goossens nods. What on earth can he say about international business? His brother had told him about profitable investments in Colombia. Or was it Bolivia? Quick, quick, before she gets up and has gone outside, perhaps he can make some pronouncement about the food industry in general, but what?

'Oh, America,' he says.

She stands up. He puts his over-confident fingers, all five, on her inner arm; it is warm and sweaty.

'As it happens, there's a rehearsal of my Cybele this evening at St Servatius. Why don't you come along? There's nothing special on television this evening – the best is a documentary about Van Gogh on Channel 2, but it's made by Americans so we know what to expect, don't we?'

'What can we expect?'

He is embarrassed for a moment. He could go on and on about the ways transatlantic culture is crushing the efforts of our own programme makers. But she wants to leave. 'The members of Concordia and myself in particular would be extremely honoured. If you have time, of course.' He tries to smile invitingly at the woman whose sweet musky perfume permeates him.

'Perhaps,' says Sibylle Ghyselen. 'Why not?'

'Then I'll come and pick you up at a quarter to eight.' He can hear the greasy voices of the regulars in the café near the town hall, opposite St Servatius, 'Hey, who's getting out of the Zavelgem headmaster's car? My god, it's his mistress!'

'No need. I'll find my own way. What time does it start?'

'Half past eight. The members prefer to eat beforehand.'

'Perhaps,' she says.

Headmaster Goossens is jubilant. He must calm down. 'My piece is, of course . . . you have to approach it as a rhapsody of course, it contains elements that, if one isn't accustomed to the style and if one doesn't know the background . . . I mean, one could quickly find it bombastic, that is to say, the thoughts and images could perhaps seem too large for the content. . . .'

He is in danger of running away with himself, but he detects something of Martin's arrogance in her expression. It is like when the boy sometimes seems to be preoccupied in class, disconnected from the other children, the room, the drone of noun declension, and without moving a muscle he absents himself from them, from Headmaster Goossens too.

'Actually,' he says, 'the piece also has a connection with you.'

'What did you say?' Aha. The witch is intrigued. Because it concerns herself.

'The title. Cybele. My main character is called Cybele.'

'And?'

'Sibylle. Cybele.'

'Coincidence.'

'Yes, eh?'

'And what sort of a creature is this Cybele?'

'The goddess of fertility.' Don't dwell on this, since she isn't all that fertile. Only one child. And then? Didn't want any more? Miscarriage? 'She is not a nice person, but she's certainly alluring.'

'Why not a nice person?'

He wants to send Liliane out to the greengrocer for tomatoes, fennel, tobacco, Coca-Cola, and then quick, quick, unzip his fly.

'Cybele was rather authoritarian,' he says and grimaces. His unzipped fly could invoke the rituals of Cybele's priests in an exemplary didactic manner.

'Explain,' she says.

'Whenever Cybele considered anyone had offended her cult, she turned him into a lion and had him tied to her carriage.'

'The men would have loved that. Don't men always want to be lions?'

'Not I,' says Headmaster Goossens. But I do, I want to nibble at the hem of her dress.

'Oh, no?'

'She forces her priests to castrate themselves.'

'That's going too far,' says Sibylle Ghyselen.

'Or to go about dressed as women.'

'How odd,' she begins. Her mouth seems fuller, swollen. She wants to recount something about that strangeness, but she stops. Liliane comes in carrying a tray with his tea: two cheese sandwiches and Knorr tomato soup in Corry's porcelain mug with the portrait of Baden-Powell.

Martin chews a mouthful of grass. Because animals eat it and are content with it. What he had done when he fled from the rabbit shed to the orchard demanded punishment. Worse still, it demanded apologies. Because he had shouted 'Drop dead!' at his mother's mother. And so loudly that God the father must have heard it, even if he was having an absent-minded moment. And if he hadn't heard it, he would do this evening when he counted up all the sins committed in Zavelgem, when he saw on one of his holy video screens what had been going on in Martin Ghyselen's head. Which was that Gran had stumbled over a toy carelessly left lying about by the same Martin Ghyselen. She had fallen in a slow-motion flurry of arms and legs, landing on a potato peeler, the peel still curved round its blade. Gran, who had given up the Holy Ghost. What would God the father do? Send a crackle of lightning out from his index finger, pointed towards the culprit, who reads the book in bed at night with a torch? Or send his son silently at night in the form of a swordfish?

In any case, even though he didn't really mean 'drop dead', it was impolite. But how do you shout something like that politely? Like the death announcements in the newspaper? 'Gran, pass away in the peace of the Lord'? 'Gran, depart from us in all tranquillity'?

Martin comes up to the tomato plants. Richard's naked feet are sticking out, looking as though they have been chopped off by the dark green leaves. Long toes full of sand. He is snoring so heavily that the tomato above his head looks as if it will be blown right off its bristly stem.

'Hey, sluggard, lazybones, dead loss.'

Richard opens one eye. 'What time is it?' He gets to his knees. 'I must have been here quite a time.'

'Over an hour,' Martin lies.

'Chappie,' says Richard. Martin recognizes the entreaty. He shakes his head.

'No!'

'Go on. In the kitchen in the fridge. You'll be there and back in two minutes.'

'No, Richard.'

'Your Gran'll never see you. You're a swift devil.'

Martin ponders. If he agrees to Richard's request, which will be colluding with the sin of drunkenness, which turns people into stupid dangerous cattle, what can he demand in return?

Richard gets to his haunches. The tomato wobbles.

'The cross is broken,' says Martin. 'You have to make another.'

'I'll do it today. Now, what are you waiting for?'

'A new cross first.'

'Straight away.'

'A stronger one.'

'Can't the other one be mended?'

'No,' says Martin and shows him the large splinter he had put into his pocket like a reliquary.

'I'll make a new one right away. Now off you go to the kitchen.'

'No,' says Martin.

Richard swears loud and long, as he learnt to in the army.

'Don't be so hysterical, old man,' says Martin and leaves him in the sand.

Richard is now suffering pain, but what is that compared with how Miss Dora suffers? Miss Dora, her dying body, threatened by the free thinkers and their *scorn*.

Martin holds the splinter of wood up in front of him, leans forward, buzzes and zooms past the sheep who jump out of his way. His lance, his sword is not sharp enough, not long enough, but it doesn't matter. He can be smaller than a real swordfish in the same way that Jesus can be a fish. It is a *metal fair*. Like there was in the vaulted wine cellars of Rome, where the Catholics hid from Emperor Nero's police, who wanted to throw them to the lions. They drew a fish on the walls, as a signal to each other. The Catholics were the fishermen and Jesus was the fish: the largest, loveliest, strongest, slinkiest fish in all the oceans. The largest? The whale isn't a fish. The dolphin? It's too tame, a Flipper, always ready to cooperate; you can't take it seriously. The shark, well yes, but it's really vicious. No, there's no doubt about it, the swordfish is the noblest. In the picture to the left of Martin's bench in the classroom. Slippery as a submarine, a long streamlined steel balloon with spiky fins, *Xiphias gladius*. Its flesh is inedible, it never sleeps, it weighs a thousand kilos, its sword is sharper and swifter than Zorro's. It notices everything, dead fish, sick fish, wounded fish with coughs. It streaks over to them and gobbles them up. It slays whales and, although it is never hysterical, it slays ships which it thinks have disguised themselves as whales. Sometimes the point of its sword breaks, but miraculously it instantly grows back again, because it is an angel and an animal at the same time and it has to chop up sinners and tax collectors into small pieces like lightning. Dark purple in the ice cold currents under the sea.

Mum is cycling back along the road. She goes on to the terrace. And just listen, her mother's grumbling has started up. Martin creeps over to the house.

'They were blushing with shame.' (They: Richard and him.) 'I'm only telling you what I saw, Sibylle. They were caught in the act, I felt that immediately. Nowadays you hear nothing but stories of children who are abused, Sibylle, and it all comes out years later.'

He can't understand Mum. She is going to agree with her mother again.

Less than an hour later he slips inside the house and finds Mum in her bedroom. She is sitting on the edge of the bed Dad had specially made for her the first week they were married. She is leaning forward and concentrating, caressing her legs with a small electric box that makes a pleasant even hum and pulls out hairs. Bits of black fluff land on the white sheet, like stipples of the finest felt pen.

'You made me look a proper fool,' she says without glancing up. 'Mr Goossens was shocked. You made the whole thing up after that stupid "Quo Vadis" film.'

'That's not what it's called.'

'All the same. That you could make such a fool of your mother. But I'll get even with you, just you wait. And now get out of my sight.'

He disobeys her. Her stands with one foot on the open drawer of the mirror-fronted wardrobe containing all sorts of satin knick-knacks. She behaves as though she doesn't see him. His eyes burn. It is impossible for him to speak. On no account must Miss Dora be martyred during her life. She must go to the reindeer freely, happily, unblemished by Martin's treason. Mum goes to the bathroom. He follows her. He sits on the toilet seat while she looks in the mirror, feels her chin, puts oil on her eyelashes, tries on earrings and puts them away again, powders her neck. A strange woman seems to be standing there, with hollow cheeks, slimmer and taller in her shiny beige petticoat, swaying uncertainly on high heeled shoes, who says, 'What's going on between you and Richard? Gran says the two of you were together in the rabbit shed.'

'Gran is a witch.'

'And you're a downright liar.'

'Mum.'

'I'm not in the mood to bother with you now. I'll have nothing to do with liars.'

Damned tears. He rips toilet paper off, pretends to blow his nose, turns away from her, dabs at his eyes.

'Does Richard sometimes come and find you? Does he get close up to you? As if to fight?'

'No.'

'Never? Doesn't he do anything else that you don't dare say?'

'No.'

'You've been inseparable from him recently.'

'Richard is a good person. It's true he was in prison but that was because he helped women.'

She stops examining her hair roots.

'Because a sickness broke out among the women in the small town where he lived. The women couldn't walk any more, they were so weak and wasted, they couldn't get up the steps of the hospital any more. And he treated them with medicines meant for animals which he knows all about, and because it isn't allowed for people they arrested him.

Meanwhile those women were healthier than ever!'

'Martin, he was convicted because he was responsible for those women not having children.'

'Didn't those women want to have children?'

'No. And he was able to organize it with an, an operation.'

'Then. And now?'

'Now, what?'

'Do they still not want those children? If you aren't fond of your child or if you think you'd rather not see your child any more as it grows up, then you're better off not having any children.'

'There are laws. . . .' says Mum, but Gran comes in, sighing, with piles of bath towels in her shrivelled arms. She says that men who have studied at public expense and who perform such practices should go to the electric chair immediately.

'Which practices?'

'You'll hear about them when you're older.'

'Must Richard go to the electric chair?'

'No exceptions, no political intrigue, immediate trial and finish.'

'Mother,' says Mum. She puts on a white silk dress, peers surreptitiously in the mirror, as though she is being spied on. If you counted up all the hours women spend looking at themselves in the mirror, it would be as long as the life of a six-year-old child. Where's Mum going? Why doesn't she give advance warning that she's going to be out for a whole evening, so that he can prepare himself for it? Martin flops into the centre of the large bed where one year ago, no less, on Sundays he was still able to lean against Dad, a warm hairy Dad who listened to the Language Debate on the radio and sometimes laughed out loud. Martin sometimes laughed along with him to please him. But what is there to laugh at if words change their meaning, if words become ridiculous because they resemble each other? Martin can't laugh at things that change, such as this bed, which has changed since Dad no longer lies in it.

'Gran, when it's cold, which metal feels warm to you?'

'I haven't a clue, Martin.'

'An electric chair!'

Well, look at that, the two women don't laugh either. Jesus never laughs, unless it is very quietly to the little children who come to him. And it's never his words that change, but he himself, into a fish, into bread, and so on. He is a vine too, but God knows what that means.

'Where are you going, Mum?'

'None of your business.'

Martin saunters across to the staircase and then dashes down to the kitchen silently, as though between caves in the deepest water. The two women will be busy for a while yet, Gran grousing and Mum dolling herself up. He opens the food cupboard with utmost caution. The door squeaks; he holds his breath, but there is no sound from upstairs. He finds the sugar. The only problem is, which one? Granulated flows nicely, but perhaps it doesn't dissolve as quickly. Brown sugar is better for putting on those hideous matzos. Castor sugar it is, just right for strawberries, waffles and revenge. He folds a crude cone out of a page of *The Standard*, pours the sugar faultlessly into it and closes the container. Carefully he tiptoes across the black stone floor and out to the garage. He thinks he can hear Richard snoring far away in the tomatoes. He goes up to the BMW, opens the flap, gets the petrol cap off easily. He must be sure to wash his hands thoroughly with soap afterwards, because of the smell. The wreckage complete, he walks away towards the sheep, bolt upright, with large strides, hands at the ready beside the two revolvers on his hips. Like Clint Eastwood, who (just like Jesus) never has children in his films, but definitely leaves forty-seven or forty-eight dead bodies behind him (Martin had counted them by slowing down and stopping the video) in *A Fistful of Dollars*.

The BMW gives out a few metres before the top of the hill, from where she can see the town, the steeples of St Servatius, the chimneys of Olympia. For five whole minutes Sibylle furiously turns the ignition key and treads on the accelerator.

(*'It's so easy to learn how a car works. Just study the diagram,' says Gerard.*)

She finds half a bar of chocolate in the glovebox. Plain. Martin doesn't like milk. She could walk home. Three quarters of an hour. There are no passing cars, of course. Saturday. Out of petrol? The warning light isn't on.

The shadows over the countryside are turning a deep blue, as though painted. Gerard's lime tree is visible far away against the horizon, its crown like an extravagant parasol. Two peasant women come past, don't greet her, think she's waiting for a lover, to have it off in the car. She'll see *Cybele* later, with the priests who emasculate themselves and walk about dressed up as women.

Own fault. Fat lump.

Gerard said, 'A child can learn it. In a couple of hours, a child can learn how a car's put together.'

'I'm not a child.'

'That's no answer.' He got angry, flushed deep red. She liked seeing him like that most of all: helpless with rage, beyond the boundary of his coolness, his haste, his authority. His rare outbursts were a contrast to the musty days in the country, the monotonous seasons and languid animals, where the growing child was the only counter rhythm; those were the moments when she felt she was alive. What she wanted, and what she now had in abundance, were the fractures and shards, disclosure of a different, splintered light whose source you couldn't see. Like the reflection from the bedside lamp on that particular night, in the mirror inside the open door of the wardrobe.

They had been to the Mayor's Ball together.

She had worn her midnight-blue silk dinner jacket against his wishes. The ladies, furiously angry and admiring, had called out how elegant, how chic, how young she looked. Gerard had concurred with this while he calmly scrutinized acquaintances to see who might reveal something about the likely implications of the new town council's left-liberal coalition. Later on, un-characteristically, he drank much too much champagne. The coalition was evidently good news. He chatted excitedly, made risqué compliments to the ladies. She also liked him best like that because, in contrast to his usual ways, he did not behave as though he understood and controlled everything, even the most resistant, mutable, volatile, fleeting and yet precious things.

In the Porsche he sang along with the radio at the top of

his voice, and when he got out he was drunker than she had ever seen him. She had to push him up the stairs to the bedroom, where she said, 'Kneel, kneel before your mistress!' and he did so, with an imbecile juvenile guffaw, and clawed at her ankle. She stepped aside.

'Lie on the bed,' she commanded in a flat voice. 'Eyes closed, slave!'

Did he already understand what was then rising up inside her like a revelation, like an illusory but urgent solution to their life together, which had been grafted onto the stale, monotonous seasons? And if he did understand it, why didn't he resist it, why did he say nothing? She switched off the ceiling light and put the bedside lamp on. She rummaged furiously in the bottom drawer of the wardrobe and found stockings, suspender belt and a belt. Her heart pounding, she thought: Lucky he's thin, so I don't have to think up any impossible, exotic inventions. She tossed the other things she kept in the wardrobe onto the bed, next to his face. His features were clamped in a sweet grin never seen during the day, never in their whole time together, a mask whose only movement was the jaw muscles when he felt her fingers on his shirt, his shoes, and then on his naked body.

'Eyes closed,' she whispered, unnecessarily because he already obeyed. She pulled him up by his shoulders and propped him upright to fasten the bra hooks.

'Quiet,' she said, although he made no sound. She assumed there would be limits to his obedience so she bound a satin Indian scarf over his eyes, impatiently now. She completed her preparations busily, almost playfully: her blonde wig from seven years ago, the gold earrings, the deep ruby-red lipstick on his trembling lips, applied as carefully as if she was making herself up, foundation cream to cover the birthmark on his shoulder, the black-sided briefs that made her giggle silently, the criss-cross of the absurdly tight belt cutting into his pelvis where his hips stuck out, the gold sandals that were too small, so she crushed his curled toes into them and laced the straps tight, making him grunt. And

89

finally, as an afterthought, she draped a purple see-through tunic over him which reached down to his navel.

Then she pulled him off the bed like a bridegroom, her hands as clammy as his. The sleeve of the tunic tore from the rough movement. She led him over to the mirror and hid behind him, so that he could be seen in his strange entirety, a defenceless, blindfold creature which he never could have become without her intervention, her creation.

'You're beautiful,' she said. She was exhausted, as though she had been climbing up and down hills non-stop for three quarters of an hour. 'Very beautiful,' she said. The sheep could be heard grazing outside. A pigeon on the roof. Then he untied the blindfold, which was soaked with sweat. She thought she had made his eyes up. She arranged the tangled blond hair from behind him.

'No,' he said softly. 'No, Sibylle.'

'But yes,' she said. 'Why not?'

He made a guttural sound as though he was going to be sick.

A thick mist is fast descending over the valley, billowing out from the woods. Sibylle feels cold. It was then that she lost him, in the matte, old-gold light reflected in the mirror. She had never had him. Why did she ever marry him? Because he could play tennis well and dance? Because Lieve and Astrid found him attractive? Because of the flamboyant strength with which he reigned over his factories, the same strength he used when he struck her that night until he dislocated his tennis-playing hand?

They drove to Hasselt the next day because they had to sign a document at the notary; one of Gerard's unfathomable deals. They had not exchanged a word the whole morning. He stared ahead, skimming past belligerent swaying lorries, his knuckles as white as paper in his driving gloves.

His resentment and his heaviness of heart enveloped

her, like the tentacles of an animal that was both jellyfish and hairy. She wanted to jump out of the car, under the lorries which whizzed along making the sound of the surf.

'Go on now, boy,' she said. 'Can't you just forget it? It was a trifle, a little game.' She renounced her triumphant efforts.

'I don't wish to speak to you any more.'

'But what have I done wrong? It really wasn't intented to hurt you!'

'Oh, yes it was. It was to laugh at me. Like you do day in, day out. I don't intend to ruin my life any longer with anyone who has such contempt for me.'

She did have contempt for him then.

'Drop dead,' she said.

'You'll be hearing from my lawyer,' he said when Hasselt came into view.

Headmaster Goossens sticks one hand up in the air like a policeman; he spreads the other hand over his face. The male members of Concordia stop, unevenly, unmelodiously, in the middle of the chorus.

'Gentlemen,' says Headmaster Goossens, 'confrontation with total inanity is giving me an unbearable headache. Ten minutes' break.'

Concordia is silent. Their conductor is not his usual self. He is moody. He has already snapped at his assistant, Mrs Veremans, and growled at the pianist.

Headmaster Goossens goes over to the aisle, where a bar has been set up, its counter resting over the marble and stone gravestones of 17th-century prelates set into it. He sips his Pale Ale and reads: 'Pray for the soul of the Reverend Baeckelant'.

'Child, I fancy a pickled herring,' he says to Mrs Veremans.

'With onions, Headmaster?'

'With an extravagant quantity of onions.' He watches her confer with three ladies by the porch. ('Artists are unpredictable.' 'They're not like us.' 'They're like pregnant women, actually.' 'Hurry, Mrs Veremans.')

He crams the herring in in two bites. The goddess has not come, won't come now, so her forsaken priest is allowed to eat onions. Though she said 'Why not?' and directed her bright, meaningful gaze straight at him, she meant the opposite: 'Why should I?' And what's more, he had allowed himself to be ensnared by an unfamiliar etiquette. When someone of her sort says in a particular tone of voice: 'You really must come round one day', the very last thing you should do is turn up. They ought to run a crash course on the subject at teachers' training college. She also said: 'How odd . . .' and wanted to admit something about herself that was strange too. Why wasn't she here, isn't she here? The rehearsal starts again. How clumsily his verses flap about beneath the cross-vaults, without rhythm, without melody! He can scan, stress the metrical feet, beat time for all he is worth, but this is going to be the flop of his life.

The governor will leave after ten minutes. Clear off after waving to the author in his jovial, plebeian manner.

The goddess will say, 'Goossens, have I had to come here to you through wind and weather for this substandard moaning? And will you point your stinking breath at someone else?'

'No, no, and once more no!' screams Headmaster Goossens. He gathers up his score, his prompt book, his annotated manuscript, his *Encyclopedia of Classical Antiquity* and his authentic 19th-century tobacco pouch.

'We're doing our best,' says Koeck, the plumber.

94

Headmaster Goossens growls, 'If this is your best, then we'd better forget this whole *Rhapsody* and the whole Culture Weekend as far as I'm concerned.'

He walks through the fan-shaped space and waves to them: 'Adios!' It echoes. He catches Concordia's murmuring. Rebellious? Distressed? Full of awe? ('What a temperament!' 'He reminds me of Karajan, so egocentric.')

Outside he considers whether or not to telephone Sibylle Ghyselen. But he has heard Martin Ghyselen saying in the playground that they have an answering machine at home. His voice will sound subservient, self-seeking, even if he doesn't want it to, could always be used as evidence on tape. 'Unwise, Willy,' he says, and gets on his moped.

The lights of Zavelgem glimmer in the distance. He could stroll down to the Golden Hen just for a little while. Play cards or a game of darts. It would be instructive. After all, you have to get your ear tuned in to the common people's idiom. Shakespeare did that for sure. But not this evening. This is the goddess's evening, even though she hasn't turned up. He will reflect upon her during the broadcast of the Gap-Briançon stage.

Then he sees her car, an abandoned, elegant silhouette with the left front door wide open. Would she be lying injured, murdered in a ditch? How will he manage to get her to the hospital in town on his moped? The key isn't in the ignition. In the glovebox he finds cigarettes, Tampax, half a shrivelled apple, sweets stuck together. Was she dragged out of the car by a couple of immigrant workers? He hardly dares to move. But he can't stay here either. Flashlights could come on at any moment – a pack of reporters from *The Evening News* could spring out of nowhere. 'School head at corpse of raped woman.' He circles round the BMW, terrified. Next to one wheel he finds a little ball, a wrapper that smells of chocolate. Cold sweat runs down his face. He dashes to his moped and pedals like mad.

The Ghyselens' house and outbuildings loom up in the white mist. Watery light shines over the front door. The moped splutters. Not a sound from anyone on the first floor. Snuffling and dull thumps from the orchard. The unusually shrill doorbell.

'Headmaster Goossens,' she says, unsurprised, wearing an Arab gown, her hair wet and combed back.

'I thought, I thought,' he says rapidly. 'That something had happened. To you. I saw your car.'

She opens the door wider, invites him into the hall, which he had imagined to be more magisterial. He doesn't care for the lily wallpaper. She speaks quietly and calmly.

'My car gave up on me. And you were concerned about me? How very kind.' A large room is visible through an open door, with broad leather chairs and oriental carpets on a black stone floor, a television on without the sound.

'Were you expecting me?' she whispers.

'Of course. We were all expecting you, me in particular.'

How will he describe her face in his opus for next year's Culture Weekend, which will not be a rhapsody but probably a modern morality play? It is as after an immense sadness, when there are no tears left.

'I can't ask you in because Martin sleeps very lightly these days.'

'Oh, I'm leaving. I only wanted to make certain that. . .'

'How did the rehearsal go?'

'Ah,' says Headmaster Goossens. 'Ah, Madam.'

'Wait.' She leaves him standing there. Enormous sunflowers appear on the TV.

She returns with a huge lantern. She walks decisively towards an outbuilding, accustomed to have one trot behind her like a lapdog of a head teacher. The lower part of the walls is hidden by haystacks; the spaces between the wattle are not plastered with lime as they should be but with whitewashed cement. Folklore on the cheap. He will send her the last issue of Local History News. Anonymously. She points the lamp at a wretchedly restored oak door and then the light enters a rebuilt barn with chesterfields, an antique desk, a billiard table, heating system, an enormous hat stand made of antlers.

'Have a seat.'

He collapses into one of the chesterfields with a squelch.

'Tell me,' she says.

'There is so much to tell,' he begins wearily, but reckons he must stick to the topic of the Concordia rehearsal. Revived, he cries, 'Do you play billiards?'

'My husband.'

'In the evenings after work?'

'Three times a week with his coach.' She pushes aside a panel in the wooden wall revealing a metal rack full of audio equipment, a shelf of bottles, a small fridge, hundreds of CDs.

'Ingenious,' says Headmaster Goossens.

She asks what he would like to drink.

Recklessly he says, 'The same as you.'

'Whisky, then,' she says. She pushes a knob. He would never have thought it. Satie. Background music for commercials: dog food, mineral water. The clinking of ice cubes.

'Cheers!'

'Shalom,' says Headmaster Goossens. She looks Pre-Raphaelite, or would do with floral garlands in her hair, draped in brocade.

She listens to Satie, jingles, icicles.

'I think I recognize Ciccolini,' he says. 'Personally I find him rather slovenly, certainly if you compare him with Reinbert de Leeuw.'

'Oh do dry up, man.'

She goes and sits on the edge of the desk; she makes the ice cubes tinkle in her square, heavy crystal glass.

Headmaster Goossens dabs his face with his handkerchief – a clean one luckily. Dear Liliane.

'I have been thinking about it, Madam. About the

situation. Our Martin is definitely going through an identity crisis. The perverse-polymorph stage, with maximum
susceptibility. . . .'

'Please. Not about Martin.'

He must calm down. He misses his pipe.

'The rehearsal didn't go as you wanted, I understand,'
she says.

'A rhapsody makes large demands. There is little the-
matic structure and, for a lyric drama such as mine, which
lacks the usual frame of reference. . . .'

A plop. Her sandal has fallen on to the carpet. Her
toenails are painted mother-of-pearl.

'Is it a coincidence that Cybele sounds like Sibylle?'
How she pronounces her own name, with familiarity and yet
with taste.

'Sibylle has the two i's of Willy, too.'

'Willy?'

'My first name. A coincidence, you ask? The world
seems to rest on coincidences and on necessity, if one researches
matters more closely. . . .'

'As you do?'

She is laughing at him. He clears his throat. The whisky
is working. 'We are not animals at the mercy of chance.'

'We are,' she says hoarsely.

He raises his voice to a stifled cry. 'If that's so, if you
really mean that. . . .' He shifts out of the sofa with the same
squelch as before and kneels, bends towards her leg and covers
it in kisses and licks. She opens her arms and lifts up the panels
of her white silk robe and drapes it over his head and shoulders.

'Don't you want to see me?'

She shrinks from the agony in the voice beneath her.
'Yes I do,' she says. 'Indeed. But not now.'

His rasping cheek wipes over her thighs, ascends higher.
'Think of someone else,' says the low, pained voice.

'Don't talk any more,' she says with her eyes closed.

98

The moment has come. In the old days, when he had masterminded a virtually faultless order of good and evil in his town, when the moment had come, he had said to Lippens without the least hesitation in front of the suspects, 'You see how you soften them up, Lippens. Patience. You must take up fishing, man; it's the best training.'

The man facing him had acquired a cobalt blue glow over his face; his protruding ears were pale violet.

'A tiny drop. Surely that's not too much to ask. Just one.'

'Another time, my friend.'

'At The Pig and Whistle in the marketplace, when pigs can fly,' said Lippens.

'I'll never go to The Pig and Whistle in the market-place again.' The man hit out at nonexistent mosquitoes (which swarmed up out of a mound of urine-dampened straw).

'Are there any cases of epilepsy in your family?' asked Lippens.

But the man did not reply.

'Simoens in the High Street isn't that bad as lawyers go,' said the police commissioner. 'He'll give you a special fixed price. Shall I phone him?'

'It isn't worth it.'

For the first time in a long while the police commissioner looked at his watch and pulled his cuffs down until they were even. 'I'll wager a real pint that you get life.'

'Death,' said Lippens. 'No doubt about it.'

'It is my right to lie,' said the man grumpily.

The police commissioner looked over his notes. 'Do you know what's bugging me? Not that you're lying, but that you're keeping quiet about something very particular, and about that specific hole in the story. Did you go straight home after The Little Rose, Rustica, Margriet? There's a hole there. You didn't go directly along the main road. Perhaps you and your drunken balls fell asleep in a cornfield. It could be, but you don't say so. You do have the right to explain this in your own time, after scheming with your defence counsel, but you know me a little bit, and I want to know.'

The tongue appeared, far beyond the long, sharp teeth. It was violet too.

'Now it could also be that you retraced your steps after your last stop at Margriet (I must speak to her about it again anyway; there would have been enough customers to confirm that she'd served you four, five, six drinks even though you were completely plastered). To the village. And then you would have had to pass the Ghyselens' villa.'

'I wanted to hang myself,' said the man. 'From Mr Gerard's big tree. But I had no rope.'

100

'You could have used your trouser cord.'

'I didn't think of that.'

'You think we'll swallow that?' cried Lippens cheerfully.

'But why did you want to hang yourself? Up to that point you hadn't done anything wrong.'

The man growled something and then, also for the first time in a long while, directed his wide open turquoise eyes at the police commissioner, who thought: The moment has come: the overwhelming desire for surrender is winning. He fetched a hipflask of thirty-five per cent Balegem gin out of his desk drawer, unscrewed the top and held it out. The man took three large gulps, swayed on his hips, held the flask tightly in his lap.

'I'll talk if your policeman leaves,' he said.

'If that's it,' said Lippens. 'If you need me, Commissioner, I'll be opposite.' He tapped encouragingly on the man's skull. 'Do your best!'

The police commissioner pushed the REC button on the tape recorder that was built into his desk cupboard. This evening he will let his wife hear the cassette in bed. She will listen to it with bated breath. 'It's the only pleasure left to me. The feeling that I can empathize a bit with you, Dirk.'

(*A surprisingly calm voice.*) 'Yes, yes, as you say, retraced my steps. Past farmer Romein's field. As you say. Not directly. Why? There are so many whys. God sends you what you can endure. But that particular why? I'll come to it. Retraced my steps and, as you say, went past the villa. Except it isn't a villa. They call it their farm. Even though it's been done up for millions it's still a farm. They think. Why? Because I didn't want to wake Julia at home, didn't want to have a row. Not that she would start a row, my Julia, but she drinks too much, and that's my fault too. She says it's better if she keeps up with me. Otherwise she's so lonely. There's something in that. She's always cold, too. Richard, there's a draught. Richard, you didn't close the front door, must the neighbours hear everything? What is there to hear, silly arse? So I thought it would be better if I slept in the barn, so that I could make a fresh start straight away the next day at dawn. At dawn.'

(*Sound of a fighter jet, buzz of policemen in the corridor.*)

'And I see light in Mr Gerard's room. I thought the little one was wandering about there, but that was odd because he needs his night's rest. Especially as no one is allowed into Mr Gerard's room. It's dusted and mopped every other day by Irene. Because you never know if Mr Gerard might come back unexpectedly. I was convinced it must be the little one because he's been odd recently. All he can think of is Jesus and Christ.'

(*Sound of a door. A young policeman says: 'Excuse me.' The high-pitched girl's voice says: 'Can't you damn well knock?' – 'I'm sorry, Commissioner.'*)

'Why? Because of the little one. Otherwise I would've gone straight to the barn. But there was that light. Otherwise I wouldn't have gone back there, to damnation.'

(*Coughing.*)

'I held on to the trees. Went from tree to tree. Past the sheep. There was a chink in the curtains. That light came from there. They should have put the light out, there was enough moonlight. They didn't hear me. Not at any point. I think I know who that chap was, but I'm not going to swear to it, I'm not going to drag anyone innocent or guilty down into the abyss with me. They were at it; what more is there to say? It's always the same. It's the same for anyone who sees it through a chink in the curtains. Not for them who's doing it, at least I don't think so. You can often think and act as though it's the first time. I went on watching. She was as red as a tomato. I wanted to go away and not go away. The main thing was, I. . . .'

(*The girl's voice, lower than before: 'The main thing was you what?'*)

'I was very turned on by it. It hasn't happened to me

in years. I'd already said adieu to the game. Adieu and merci, not for me thanks; I'd rather not. And I was ashamed of that. I like her, Madam Sibylle. I never would have touched her, but at that moment I would have. At that moment, it's ugly to say so, Mr Commissioner, but I would've done it to a sheep. Ashamed, yes indeed, ashamed, but I also wanted to smash the window in and do a mischief with a sledge hammer in that room. God sends what we can endure, but that went beyond the bounds of endurance. Then I left the two of them. Looked for a rope in the straw, but I was too drunk. Tried to get back on my bike again.'

(*Sound of two cars, each with a loudspeaker: the election campaign.*)

'Went home.'

(*'Along the main road?'*)

'I wouldn't swear to it. In the direction of home, that's all.'

(*Sound of a fighter jet. A radio, pop song.*)

'She wasn't pleased, and I must say that I – that I . . .'

(*The man weeps.*)

' . . . that I wasn't careful. Usually I take my shoes off, try not to bump into the chairs, there are three of them, but you still need to watch out. But I did bump into the stove, bumped into the cupboard, knocked into the bedroom door. She didn't say a word, just made coffee.'

(*The man blows his nose, clears his throat.*)

'I've always handed over my money. Always respected her. Even when she got mad at me. She's an orphan child and never learnt anything. I always treated her kindly. In my way. Not like other men do their wives. Because I'm no longer a man. No longer was. Except for last night. I even thought of me with Julia in her nightdress. But she started on about a suit that she'd seen in C & A. I say, "Girl, what's that going to cost?" She says, "Oh, Richard, we only live once." I say, "But girl, what in God's name do you want with a suit?" "For going into town," she says. I say, "But girl, who looks at you in town now?" "It's true," she says.

'And because that is true I get a headache and I start looking for my bag where I keep my pills and aspirins. My bag from before, with my instruments, which I'll never part with. She sees me looking and she says, "Your bag's under the bed, it was in the way, I'll get it for you." And I say, "Damn right you'll get it, and I'm the one who's going to give it to you." She starts laughing. "You?" she says. "That'll be front page news!" On top of my headache and my anger. She didn't mean it badly, Julia; it was really meant to make me laugh. But I wasn't in the mood for laughing. And then I gave her a little shove.'

('A little shove?')

'A little shove. "Ow," she said, "you hurt me." "Hurt, hurt, what do you know about hurting!" I shouted. She said, "Sweetie, I do know, but you mustn't hit me." But it was too late. I boiled over. All my anger from those years. Not anger against her, certainly not against my sweetie, I'll stake my life on that. And then I punched her again and again until I couldn't any more, and fell unconscious. And now Mr Commissioner, I'd like to sleep a bit, if that's allowed.'

(*But when you fell unconscious, before then I mean, was she still alive?*)

'Of course she was still alive.'

(*'Was she bleeding?'*)

'Of course she was bleeding.'